"Whoever awarded you this training scholarship needs his head read! You are nowhere near experienced enough to even be in this club!"

Anda Barnes is miserable. She's given up six whole weeks of her summer holidays to train at a top London gym club, and now everything is going wrong! Everyone has praised Anda's natural talent before, but now she's beginning to wonder if she has *any*. Ian Barst, the trainer at the club, can find nothing but fault with everything she does.

Anda is stunned — and she hasn't even got her mum or dad with her to make her feel better. She's staying with her aunt, and whilst she gets on all right with her cousin David, she never seems to be on the right side of Aunt Moira.

Perhaps Anda should give up and go home; back to the friendly Ferndale Gym Club where she knew what she was doing; back to Hooty Cottage where she lives. Perhaps Anda hasn't got what it takes to be a gymnast after all...?

Sequel to the bestselling
The Little Gymnast

Somersaults

Sheila Haigh

SOMERSAULTS

Hippo Books
Scholastic Publications Limited
London

Scholastic Publications Ltd.,
10 Earlham Street, London WC2H 9RX, UK

Scholastic Inc.,
730 Broadway, New York, NY 10003, USA

Scholastic Tab Publications Ltd.,
123 Newkirk Road, Richmond Hill,
Ontario L4C 3G5, Canada

Ashton Scholastic Pty. Ltd.,
P O Box 579, Gosford, New South Wales,
Australia

Ashton Scholastic Ltd.,
165 Marua Road, Panmure, Auckland 6,
New Zealand

First published by Blackie and Son Limited, UK, 1987

Published in paperback by Scholastic Publications Ltd., 1988
Copyright © Sheila Haigh, 1987

ISBN 0 590 70787 6

All rights reserved
Made and printed by Cox and Wyman Ltd., Reading, Berks.
Typeset in Plantin by Collage (Design in Print), Longfield Hill, Kent.

Contents

1

A Chance to Train in London

"She'll hate it."

Lynne twisted round in the seat of the van to catch a last glimpse of her daughter Anda standing alone in the long London street. She looked small and brave but somehow forlorn as she waved goodbye.

"I feel terrible, Bill. We can't leave her!"

Traffic closed in behind them. Lynne could no longer see Anda.

"We've done the right thing," said Bill firmly. His ancient van, christened Murgatroyd, shuddered to a halt at the traffic lights.

"She'll be running home in a week," said Lynne.

"Oh, you know Anda. She's tougher than that, especially over gymnastics. She'll survive."

"I shan't," said Lynne, close to tears. "I know I moan at her but I'm going to miss her so much. Hooty Cottage will be like a morgue."

"Yes, I know what you mean." Bill scratched his beard thoughtfully, then panicked as the lights changed. "This traffic's really throwing me. Don't talk to me, Lynne. Let me drive, OK?"

"OK," sighed Lynne, sadly considering the three hundred kilometres that would soon separate her from Anda.

"A lot depends," said Bill at the next traffic lights, "on whether she can stand Moira, and what her cousin David is like. Last time I saw him, he was a supercilious brat."

With mixed feelings, Anda watched Murgatroyd disappear into the traffic.

She had won a training scholarship in gymnastics, and her coaches, Christie and John, had arranged for her to spend her summer holidays training with a leading London club. She was having to stay with Bill's divorced sister, Moira, and her cousin David, whom she hardly knew.

"And I don't know how you'll get on with Moira," Bill had warned. "She's not like me."

At least her parents were honest. They didn't try to wrap it up.

Anda turned to face Moira, who waited at the top of the steps. The house stood in a long tree-lined street. Across the road were blocks of flats, and one gigantic office block full of little square windows, which Anda immediately christened "the Waffle". Between the buildings stretched a flyover beaded with traffic.

The London sky was reduced to a piece of jigsaw. At home it was circular, like an upturned blue bowl, its edges gold or silver according to the time of day. What a silly thing to be homesick about, so soon and so painfully.

"Aren't you coming in?" asked Auntie Moira brightly.

Anda looked down at her shoes. One had a piece of mud from the Hooty Stream still on it. Her only relic of home, she thought, picking it off reluctantly.

Cream-painted pillars and walls bordered cream-painted steps. Good for practising on. Straddle lifts and handstands on the pillars. I could really frighten Auntie Moira, thought Anda. Then she remembered she was a proper gymnast now, not a tearaway doing handstands in the street. She followed Auntie Moira inside.

"I was just looking round," said Anda. "It's so different from home."

"Quite," agreed Auntie Moira. "It's civilized. Bill always did want to play Tarzan — I suppose he's got a couple of tame lions in the garden?"

Anda smiled.

"No. Only two goats. And my cat, Bella. And twenty-six chickens. Oh, and an orphan lamb we've bottle-fed for the farmer. And Julienne's guinea pig, and a..."

"Don't tell me any more!" Auntie Moira shuddered.

Anda looked at her critically, taking in the permed hair, the elegant clothes, the carefully made-up face. Beneath the make-up Auntie Moira's eyes seemed oddly familiar.

"You look just like Gran," Anda said. "Only slimmer."

"Thank you! Well, I am her daughter. You look a bit like her yourself."

"No I don't," said Anda crossly. She had toffee brown hair and toffee brown eyes. Her features were elfin, like her mother's, people told her. She even looked like a gymnast, her friend Julienne used to say enviously.

"How is Gran? I haven't seen her for ages," said Auntie Moira.

"She's OK."

Auntie Moira was obviously trying to make bright conversation. I suppose she thinks I'm homesick, thought Anda. I suppose she regards me as a little kid really.

"Do you mind if I call you Moira instead of Auntie?" she suggested. "I call Mum and Dad Lynne and Bill."

"All right," Moira agreed, but she didn't look too pleased. Anda heard her mutter under her breath something about "trendy kids".

"I'm not trendy. And I'm not tidy either," Anda warned. She half wanted to stir it, to rebel at the strangeness. Thick, immaculate carpet. Gleaming chair legs. And net curtains! Totally different from Hooty Cottage, with its sun-warmed stones, threadbare rugs and happy chickens.

Moira was determined to avoid any confrontations. They would probably come later, when Anda had settled down, she thought. Bill had warned her that Anda covered her shyness with chatter, usually saying the wrong thing. If she were mine, Moira thought, I'd dress her in decent clothes, not tatty jeans. A pity she seems so tough and earthy.

"I'll bet you can't wait to start at the gym,"

said Moira as Anda followed her upstairs.

"Well — yes and no. It's not easy, suddenly having a new coach. I get on really well with John and Christie at Ferndale."

"Oh, you'll be all right at Mollins. I don't know who your coach will be but —"

"Ian Barst."

"Yes — I don't know him. But it's a fabulous place, Anda. They've got several beams, an enormous foam pit — that's new, David says. Did you know he trains there too?"

"No!" exclaimed Anda. "I'd no idea! Is he a gymnast too, then?"

"Oh yes, he's quite good. He's into Sports Acrobatics at the moment."

"Sports Acrobatics? What's that?"

"They work in pairs, or sometimes threes — you know, balancing on each other's shoulders and things like that. He'll be home any minute now. I'd better go and get his tea. Can you manage your unpacking?"

Left alone in the sugar-pink bedroom, Anda had time to think. The afternoon was stifling hot. Behind its frilled curtains, the window was tightly shut. Anda stood up on a pink velvet ottoman and attacked the window. She shifted the catch with much aggressive thumb work and flaking of pink paint, then she tried to slide the lower half up. It wouldn't budge. Better get up higher, she thought. Off came her shoes, and soon she was balancing barefoot on the narrow window ledge.

The paint was sealed across the crack where the window was supposed to slide. A knife.

That's what she needed. Make yourself at home, Moira had said. So Anda padded into the bathroom and found some nail scissors. She picked away at the seal of the paint. In five minutes the window was loose enough to rattle. She reached up, hooked her finger over the top and tugged. No. She tugged again, feeling she would suffocate. It still wouldn't budge.

"What on earth are you doing?"

The imperious voice made Anda leap backwards, off the window sill. Hooty Cottage would have shuddered, but Moira's carpetted house didn't even creak.

"I'm David. Hi."

"Hi."

David strolled into her room. Surely he wasn't going to shake hands! He was. She looked down at the broad clean hand clutching her suntanned one. Know people by their eyes, Bill always said. So Anda looked searchingly at David's eyes. They were really pine forest. Green, with flecks of mischievous light. He looks fun, Anda thought instantly.

David was taller than her. He wore a green and black track suit, clean training shoes and had a sports bag slung from one shoulder.

"I was trying to get the window open."

"Fat chance," said David, knowing full well the window had never been opened. "Whatever for?"

"I need some fresh air."

"Fresh air." David raised his eyebrows. "You mean carbon-monoxide fumes. I should leave it shut."

I told her not to open it, he could afterwards say to Mum. David leaned in the doorway, watching Anda struggling with the window. He couldn't help being fascinated by her elfish agility, even though he'd made up his mind to hate her. He didn't want some wonder kid invading his home and outshining him at gymnastics. Let her stay in the country and rot, he'd thought angrily.

CRACK!

Paint splintered. Cords snapped and the window slid down, bang. A green and glittering crack shot across the glass.

David melted away. Let her go and own up by herself, he thought. Why should he get involved?

"Oh *no*."

Anda screwed up her whole face, then slowly opened her eyes and looked. She felt as if her chest had opened and her feelings flown out like birds and flown in again.

"What on earth can I do?" she muttered desperately. "Hide it?"

Sooty wind lifted the net curtains and revealed the crack. Anda thought about Murgatroyd rattling home down the motorway, with Bill and Lynne inside. Why do I always break something? she agonised. She wished Moira would come up and discover the broken window. That would be easier than actually having to tell her.

She listened at the top of the stairs. David was telling his mum, with relish, about an accident someone had had at the gym club.

"And there was blood everywhere..."

"Not when I'm making tea, David, please!"

Didn't David know she had broken the window? Why hadn't he offered to help, or at least tell Moira for her! Anda felt annoyed with him. She hoped Moira wouldn't be too cross about the window, but if she was, well — Anda didn't have to stay, did she? What had she got to lose? Only her entire future as an Olympic gymnast!

That thought made her apologize nicely instead of defiantly.

"I'm sorry, I've broken the window," she said.

Moira bristled in disbelief.

"You've been here five minutes and already you've broken a window! Which window? How?"

"I'm really very sorry. I was trying to open it."

"Oh, tough luck. I did tell you not to open it. What a shame," said David with an ill-concealed smirk.

Ignoring him, Anda tried to explain while Moira tried to hide her annoyance.

"I desperately needed some fresh air. I didn't know it would break — it's only cracked anyway."

"It's all right. Don't worry, Anda," Moira said.

"I'm terribly sorry. Really. I'll pay for it if you like. Dad gave me a fiver," Anda offered, digging into her pocket.

"It's OK."

14

But it obviously wasn't as OK as all that. Windows and new paint and carpets mattered to Moira. Anda retreated upstairs. Moments later David crossed the landing red-faced and vanished into his room with a slam. He opened the door again and glowered at Anda.

"I copped the blame for that! So you watch it, Anda-country-bumpkin-Barnes!" he hissed. "Especially as I'm taking you to gym club tomorrow. I might just lose you on the Underground!"

Anda caught a glimpse of an expensive stereo and a computer in his room before he shut the door. No wonder Bill said David was spoilt!

She sat down on her bed. The thought of the London Underground frightened her. She'd only been on it once. But it wouldn't do to let David know that. He'd have a birthday! She'd have to be bolshy and pretend she didn't care. There was no one else to take her to gym club. Moira worked every day as a receptionist.

Half-heartedly, Anda considered unpacking. She undid the string from her bursting suitcase. After some deep digging she extracted photographs of Hooty Cottage, the goats, her friend Julienne and her beloved cat Bella. She'd begged to be allowed to take Bella with her to London, but had finally agreed that the cat would be happier, and safer, at home. Anda pressed her cheek against the cold photograph of Bella's furry face. Now I can only see your image, she thought. I can't touch your lovely fur or play with you.

Outside, the London evening was hot and

golden grey. I'll go for a walk, thought Anda, like I do at home. At home she was free to muck about by the Hooty Stream, climb trees, or run high up on the heather-covered moors. Leaving her case chucked on the bed in a tangle of sleeves and string, she skipped downstairs and out into the street.

She felt suddenly free, jogging down the long street past tree trunks and parking meters, in and out of people walking home from the station. She found a path leading up on to a high footbridge, and ran up to it to watch the trains. The speed and sootiness of London was oddly exciting.

This will be my special place, Anda decided, thinking she would often climb the railway bridge to see fragments of sunset, and watch the huge jumbo-jets knifing down towards the airport. Maybe she would even befriend a pigeon. Anda craned over to watch a line of them settling down to roost.

And then she saw the girder.

It stretched tantalizingly across a canal alongside the railway, the perfect beam, but dangerously high. Anda imagined dancing on it, daringly trying a roll or a cartwheel. No, I musn't. But I might, one day! That did not scare her so much as the thought of walking into a strange gym club tomorrow morning, alone and friendless. But I'm good, she thought arrogantly. Christie and John thought so anyway. Ian Barst is bound to be pleased with me. She slowly wandered back through the leafy streets. Mentally Anda prepared herself for being lost on the Tube tomorrow. She would not get lost! Gran had given her a map of the London Underground. She would study it, and make sure she knew where to go! She was unprepared for the outburst from Moira when she arrived back.

"Where have you *been?* David's out searching for you!"

"For a walk."

"A *walk!*"

"Yes. Why not?"

Moira seemed momentarily speechless. She spluttered to find words.

"But you can't — You don't — You can't just *walk* out of a strange house and disappear! I was frantic!"

"I do at home."

"But it's different here. This is *London.*"

"Yes. I do know it's London."

Moira glared at her.

"Are you being insolent?" she growled.

Their eyes met beadily.

"No," said Anda.

"Because one insolent brat is quite enough for one day," snapped Moira. "I've already had David thinking he can manipulate everyone. And now you…"

The words buzzed past Anda like a swarm of bees. I'm hard enough not to care, she thought angrily. What's Moira to me? But she was close to tears, wishing she was at home. I want to be a gymnast, she thought, but I don't want to live here in this carpeted palace with Moira watching my every move. There are no animals

17

here. There's nothing to love, and I daren't put anything down anywhere in case I make a mess! What would Bill do? Climb down and apologize, probably.

So Anda said, "Sorry, Moira. I do realize I should have told you where I was going. I'll go and unpack now."

Moira tossed her head, exasperated.

"Just like Bill," she said under her breath.

Anda walked upstairs. Go home. Go home, she kept thinking. But you'll never be a gymnast if you do!

2

I'll Show Him

Morning brought a headache, and a pink pigeon crooning on her window sill! Anda crept out of bed, moving like a ghost until she could almost have touched the pigeon. It waddled away, then stopped, tilting its head to look at Anda through the cracked window pane.

"Hi little pigeon," she said softly. "I wanted a friend like you! Are you hungry?"

The pigeon made a croaking noise in its throat.

"I'll sneak you up a biscuit. You wait and see!"

She looked at her watch. Eight! They were training at nine. And David had threatened to lose her on the Tube!

She dressed quickly in her leotard, training tights and her Ferndale purple track suit. What sort of reception would she get downstairs?

Moira was friendly.

"Hello Anda. You do look smart. Did you sleep well?"

"Yes thanks."

David was sprawled across two armchairs, reading a newspaper. He didn't look up. He didn't look at Anda once, but appeared to be completely engrossed in the paper while she picked at her cornflakes. She felt too nervous to eat.

"You're being really rude, David," objected Moira.

David glowered deeper into his newspaper.

Ten minutes later he and Anda set off for the Tube, both with sports bags over their shoulders. The morning was clear and warm, full of rippling leaves and traffic noise.

"Well at least we have one thing in common," said Anda, jogging to keep up with him.

"What's that?"

"Your mum doesn't have much control over you. Lynne doesn't have much control over me! Bill does, though — but only because he's kind."

David glanced briefly at her.

"Yeah, well — but I don't have my dad, do I?"

"Don't you ever see him?" asked Anda.

"Sometimes," said David. "I used to see him every Sunday when I was little and cute. Now I'm bigger he's not so interested."

Is that why he's so moody? Anda wondered. But he doesn't have to take it out on me!

David wouldn't wait for her. She scurried after him into the Underground station. Operating the slot machines with careless expertise, he bought tickets for both of them with the money Moira had given him. Without glancing at Anda, he bounded down the escalator. He's showing off, Anda thought. She flew down after him, two steps at a time, determined not to be left behind.

"Quick!" he yelled. "There's a train in now."

They pelted down the gleaming brick archways, between faces, shopping bags and legs. Anda dodged and twisted. No time to feel scared or to hesitate, as she had done on her first trip to London with Ferndale Gym Club. David leapt on to the hissing train and almost dragged Anda after him as the doors closed.

It was rush hour. Sleeve by sleeve people crammed into the train. Anda had never been so hemmed in.

"How are we going to get out?" she asked.

David actually smiled at the sight of her scared face.

"It's OK," he said. "It's always like this. You'll get used to it."

The train bolted off into darkness. Everyone swayed and long pipes streamed past the windows. Anda was terrified. Supposing the train jumped the rails and crashed in the dark tunnel. Anda Barnes, promising young gymnast, would never be heard of again! Despite her apparent composure, David noticed her frightened eyes. He felt a bit sorry.

"You're really scared, aren't you? You aren't as hard as you make out!"

"I'm OK at home," Anda said. "I could show you things that would frighten you at home."

"It's all right, I wasn't laughing at you. Come on, we get off here."

Forcing a gap through the bodies, they left the train to disappear into its tunnel. It wasn't until they were going up the escalator, smelling the fresh air at the top, that Anda started worrying about the gym club. Tired and tense, she followed David into the huge building.

White-faced, she looked up at her new coach, Ian Barst. He resembled one of the seven dwarfs, stocky with a knobbly nose and two blue gleams for eyes. The vast gym echoed around her. Blue mats and beams and bars. I feel giddy, thought Anda suddenly. I feel sick.

"I'm sorry," she began, and fainted, slap, on the wooden floor.

"Help," said David. "What on earth is wrong with her?"

Ian Barst shouted across the gym.

"Brenda! First Aid quickly, please!"

Brenda, a black girl in a green track suit, came running.

"She hasn't dropped dead, has she?" said David.

"No. Just fainted, I expect," said Brenda in her calm West Indian voice. "Poor girl. Is this the little gymnast from the West Country?"

"Yes."

"Why would she have fainted, David? Was she ill this morning?"

"I don't think so."

"Did she eat breakfast?"

"No. She might have been upset, or maybe

homesick. She hates the Tube, and Mum blew off at her last night when she'd only just arrived."

"Poor little girl!" said Brenda kindly. "How old is she?"

"Twelve."

"She doesn't look it."

"Her folks live in this isolated cottage miles from anywhere," said David. "They're really skint. And hippie types, Mum says."

The three of them crouched around Anda. Brenda wouldn't move her, except for putting a coat under her head. Slowly Anda became aware of a rumbling roaring sound in her ears. The Tube train! It had crashed! With her on it! Then voices.

"Just a straight faint."

"What caused it?"

"Maybe I rushed her along too much," said David, guiltily.

"But she ought to be fit — I mean — a gymnast!"

"Yes but — she isn't used to London."

And worse:

"She won't be able to train today," said Ian Barst, getting up on one knee.

"I will. I will. I can train," muttered Anda, coming round slowly. The man with the knobbly nose was her coach! He came sharply into focus. Then Brenda's black face which split into a beautiful smile.

"Hi," she said to Anda. "I'm Brenda. I'm the club nurse. How do you feel now? You had a nasty faint, poor Anda!"

Club nurse! Ferndale had had a box of plasters and two bottles of aspirin. Anda sat up and stared around her. This club was unbelievable! Heaps of mats, three trampolines, a foam pit, rows of beams on which girl gymnasts were already working. Next door, a specially designed vaulting room echoed to the bang of springboards. Through yet another alcove boy gymnasts were working on pommel horses and rings. Many of the gymnasts were West Indian or Oriental. There were very few white girls like herself.

"Wow," she said, taking it all in. "I wish Julienne could see this. You've got so much equipment! And so many coaches — it's vast!"

The colour slowly returned to her cheeks. She itched to get on one of those beams!

"I'll be OK now. I can train, honestly."

"No," said Brenda, and Ian Barst shook his head.

"You have a drink and a snack and rest for half an hour. No argument," he said sternly. "Low blood sugar probably."

"Go on David — you get working," said Brenda.

"Are you sure you're OK now, Anda?" David asked, looking oddly concerned.

"Yes, thanks. I'm sorry," she said with a shrug.

"I expect I shall get the blame. I usually do," he added.

"He's so neurotic, your cousin!" said Brenda, grinning teasingly at David. "He feels guilty for breathing!"

Anda frowned. David hadn't seemed that way to her. She allowed Brenda to take her into the canteen and buy her some milky coffee and a sandwich.

"I'm ravenous," she said. "I haven't eaten since yesterday's lunch at home. I was too worked up."

"Silly girl," Brenda tut-tutted. Anda felt completely at ease with her. She felt you could tell Brenda anything and she'd be sympathetic.

"What's Ian Barst like?" Anda asked.

"Tough. But OK if you get on with him. Not everyone does," warned Brenda. "I've seen more than one leave the club in tears because of him. But he's good."

"What do you mean — tough?" asked Anda. "What does he do?"

Brenda hesitated. She eyed Anda quizzically with her tea-brown eyes.

"Well —" she said, "I've seen him reduce many girls to tears."

"He won't do that to me. I'm tough too!"

"I wouldn't be too sure about that. He's a good coach — he gets results — but he's not very — aware." Brenda leaned forward confidentially. "Don't tell him I said so."

"I won't."

Brenda was definitely one to share secrets with, Anda thought. But in the weeks to come she was to find out, the hard way, exactly what Brenda meant about Ian Barst.

"If you do get in trouble, you can come to me," Brenda said. "I'm not just a nurse. I'm Lost Clothes Finder, unofficial taxi driver,

25

Distributor of Forbidden Mars Bars, and chief shoulder to cry on. So don't forget. Got to go now."

Anda finished her drink and wandered back to the gym. Two girls doing floor work smiled and said hello.

"What did you do? Crack your head?" asked one, a thin monkey-like child, all mouth and legs.

"No," said Anda, shame-faced. "I fainted."

"Are you new?"

The other girl looked Chinese or Japanese, small and stocky with dark eyes. Anda nodded, pleased to see two friendly faces.

"We're Nell and Keewong."

"I'm Anda Barnes."

She felt like adding "and I've won a training scholarship" but Ian Barst appeared beside her.

"Let's see what you can do, then," he said curtly. "Warm up and we'll start you on floor work first. Video's in there."

"Video?"

Anda had fully expected Ian Barst to ask her if she were all right. Had he forgotten she'd fainted? And video? What did that have to do with gymnastics?

"What — that room there?" she asked, seeing a door marked WARM-UP AREA. Her innocent question sent a puff of impatience steaming from Ian Barst.

"Oh, not another yokel. Show her, will you Nell?"

He swung round to talk to Keewong, who had fallen off the beam. "You aren't concentrating, Keewong."

"Show her what?" asked Nell, but Ian Barst had evidently dismissed them both as idiots.

"Video?" Anda said helplessly to Nell.

"It's OK. Come with me. He's like that with everyone, especially at first." Nell talked at great speed in broad cockney. "We've got a video-ed warm up — it puts everyone off at first but it's useful if you're warming up on your own. You'll get used to it! Where you from then, Anda? David was saying you were a hippie kid and your folk live in an old bus. Do you really?"

"No, of course not," said Anda, angry. "We live in a country cottage. David's never even seen it."

"OK. OK. Don't blow your cool."

"I wasn't."

"You're lucky!" said Nell, leading Anda into a carpetted room which had a television high up on one wall. She darted across to it and switched it on. "There you are — you've got to follow that. See you!"

She was gone, with her swift monkey grin, leaving Anda alone and bewildered. Anda wasn't sure how to take Nell. She talked so *fast*. Her arms waved and her mouth gabbled like a glove puppet. Anda couldn't decide whether Nell was mocking or friendly.

Alone and self-conscious in the huge room, Anda tried to follow the video-ed warm-up, done by an efficient, elastic girl gymnast.

Her spirits lifted as she worked. Gymnastics had a magic power to make Anda happy. Like conquering flight, it gave her a freedom beyond the reach of most humans.

But what really threw her was Ian Barst's silence.

After the warm-up he asked to watch her on the floor, beam and bars, in that order. Vaulting would have to wait until tomorrow, he said. Anda started optimistically on her floor routine, knowing it had won her the training scholarship. But every time she glimpsed Ian Barst between the tumbling runs he was stony-faced and when she had finished, he simply said,

"Right, now beam."

"Was it OK?" Anda asked anxiously, searching his face for a crack in the stone.

Ian Barst didn't answer. He didn't even look at Anda.

"Can we have your beam, Carol?" he asked a mature-looking girl who was practising.

"Sure."

"Get on with it then."

You rude man, Anda thought, already angry. She kept quiet, as she had learned to do. Gymnasts with tempers like hers were not popular with coaches!

Beam was her best apparatus. So up she went, stretching and dancing, balancing and cartwheeling for Ian Barst. Considering she hadn't done her competition routine for a month, she did well, in her opinion.

But Ian Barst remained silent. Perhaps he's flabbergasted at my talent, Anda thought. John and Christie had been. Even when she'd first joined dear old Ferndale Gym Club, not knowing anything, John and Christie had been excited and enthusiastic. Little, suntanned

Anda, dancing on the beam and flying over the vault, had been their big discovery.

"Was it OK?" she asked again.

Enragingly, Ian Barst turned away as if Anda didn't exist, and started training Nell and Keewong. Anda was amazed to see them doing double somies with apparent ease. I couldn't possibly do those, she thought. Ian Barst seemed to be OK with *them*. He was actually laughing and joking.

Sadly Anda returned to the beam and began her routine again.

"Hey, I was using that beam. If you don't mind."

She looked down at Carol's rather hostile face. It looked oddly familiar.

"Where've I seen you before?" Anda asked.

"Maybe on telly. I won the Championship at Crystal Palace last Saturday."

"Wow. Yes, you did. I did see you," said Anda, remembering. "You were great."

Carol smiled.

"Oh go on — finish your routine then," she said more kindly. "I don't envy you if Ian's testing you. He's a real pig when you first come. Believe me, Anda, I've been to hell and back in this club! But it was worth it."

Suddenly Ian Barst was behind her again.

"Now bars," he ordered.

"Well, what's the matter?" he asked aggressively as Anda hesitated.

"Nothing," Anda shrugged.

"You West Country girls are so slow," complained Ian Barst. "A Cockney kid would have been up there by now. Your reactions are half the speed of anyone else's. Is it the air down there or something? Or the way the cows amble?"

"No."

Anda had never considered herself slow! I mean — *slow* — she thought with astonishment. Me of all people!

She followed Ian Barst into the bars section, where the air seemed full of flying girls. David was there, grunting and groaning as he swung himself about on the rings.

"Don't grunt, David," his coach was saying. "It doesn't improve your performance one bit."

David paused to wink at Anda.

"Are you better now?" he called.

Anda turned.

"Yes thanks." She jerked her thumb at Ian Barst's back. "But *he* doesn't think so."

Her eyes flashed at David.

"Tough cookies," he said kindly.

Perhaps she quite liked David after all.

By the time she had adjusted the bars, and forgotten to chalk her hands, Ian Barst was bristling with impatience. His attitude unnerved Anda. She'd worked long and hard on the asymetric bars at Ferndale, and loved it. She was proud of her fearless strength and speed.

She worked for about twenty minutes, until Ian Barst called her down. To her surprise, David was standing there.

"It's nearly twelve o'clock, Anda," he said. "We've got to go soon."

The two hours had flown!

But to Anda's embarrassment, David hovered there, listening to the devastating words Ian Barst was saying to her.

"Now look here, young lady," he began, as if she were a naughty child. "Whoever awarded you this training scholarship?"

"I thought you knew!" fired Anda indignantly. "It was — "

"Yes, yes, yes, I know," he cut in. "Well, whoever the judge was, he needs his head read! You are nowhere *near* experienced enough to even be in this club!"

"What?"

Anda crumpled. It couldn't be happening! On her first day, with such high hopes! Ian Barst couldn't really be saying this to her! But he was.

She looked down at her feet. Tears hit her shoes and she didn't dare look up.

"I'm not saying you haven't got promise," he said more kindly, like a bully blustering to make amends, "but you are going to have to work very, very hard, or I'm not going to even consider training you. And if you can't take the pressure, kid, you get back to the West Country and dream your little dreams, because you won't get any success up here!"

"But what's wrong?" blurted Anda, angry enough not to care that she was openly crying. Her voice was childishly loud and David was watching!

Ian Barst sighed. He tried to be uncle-like and failed.

"I couldn't begin to tell you. We've got to go through your movements, one by one, and

31

improve them before we can get anywhere. And let's face it, you could do that in your own home club!"

Return to Ferndale, with a flea in her ear! Oh no!

"Well I *won* the training scholarship," she shouted. "And I'm not giving it up. I'm staying!"

"My, my! We are a little spitfire!"

"And if you weren't so rude and sarcastic you might get better results yourself!" yelled Anda. "I'll show you, Ian stupid Barst!"

And, quite unable to handle her anger and shock, she turned on her heel and headed for the changing room.

"I'll show him," she muttered furiously. "I'll show him."

3

One Hour of Madness

"Well, that's it. I can't go back."

Anda and David strolled towards the Tube station. Dust rose from the hot pavements. Buses roared and trains clattered. Whatever had possessed her to spend August in London?

"You can."

"I can't."

"You *can*."

"No," said Anda, still shaking inside from the episode with Ian Barst. "After what I said!"

David grinned.

"You were brilliant," he said approvingly. "Everyone was loving it. Ian Barst's had that coming to him. It's about time someone told him."

"Well I hate him already," said Anda. "I hate him. And he looks like Grumpy of the seven dwarfs!"

"I thought you were supposed to be shy!" teased David.

"Shy, maybe, but not chicken. I've got a

monster temper," admitted Anda. "I had it under control, until I met *him*."

"Come on, don't be so savage. He's hard. He'll get over it." David was being kind. He'd changed his mind about Anda since watching her standing up to Ian Barst.

"I've blown it with your mum too."

"No, you haven't."

"I'm going home," announced Anda as David bought tickets. "On the next train. And Ian Barst can keep his fancy gym club."

But how it hurt thinking of the super facilities at the gym. It was a dream gym! That foam pit she hadn't tried. The trampolines! And Ian Barst hadn't even seen her vault! *That* would show him! Or would it? Anda's confidence was too shaken to know.

"You can't do that, Anda. Don't be stupid!"

"Can't I? You watch me," threatened Anda. "I'm going straight upstairs to pack when I get in. Don't think I don't know *how* to get home, because I do. I know where Paddington Station is. I've got a map. And legs."

David laughed.

"You can't walk there, Anda!"

"I'll get a taxi then. I know how to do that, too!"

"It'll cost you a fortune! More than your rail ticket!"

"I don't care. I've got money. Gran gave me a secret tenner in case I got into trouble. It's well hidden, and," she added, "I'm not telling *you* where it is."

"I don't need your money. I can get money

any time I like," boasted David.

"You're spoilt," said Anda contemptuously.

They stood arguing on the escalator. David's pine-forest eyes were blazing.

"Don't you say that to me!" he flamed. "You don't know anything about me. *You*'re the one who's spoilt. Both your parents dote on you. So does Gran. You think you're it!"

Anda was shocked. Her parents — and Gran — were special to her. They had all followed Anda's gymnastic career loyally and backed her up. When Anda had won the training scholarship, Gran had actually cried with happiness. How would Gran and Lynne and Bill feel if she quitted now, over a silly disagreement?

"To tell you the truth, Anda," David went on in a calmer voice, "I'd like you to stay. We could have fun together through the holidays."

Anda shrugged. Perhaps David was lonely. Perhaps he needed a friend. His arrogance could be just a cover-up. Anda had compassion for all living things, whether they were kittens, hunted foxes, pigeons, or arthritic old ladies. She always rushed to help if anyone was in trouble. That was how Bill and Lynne had raised her. She'd never even been allowed to squash an ant. Perhaps that accounted for her indignant reaction to Ian Barst's criticism. *She* had been the ant that he had squashed! Standing on the long platform, Anda made a quick decision.

"I'll stay," she said. "But only because of you, not because of Ian Barst."

"Great," said David.

It was a good get-out anyway. In her heart she

didn't really want to quit. She must still face Ian Barst in the morning, but at least David was backing her.

"I know lots of places," he said enthusiastically. "We'll go down the canal this afternoon. And it's only a bus ride to the park. They've got an adventure playground. And a fair! And masses of ducks. I suppose you'll like those!"

Anda thought briefly of the girder she'd seen crossing the canal. She knew that one day she would dare to dance on it.

"You can try my computer too," said David.

"Thanks."

"We've got to fix our own lunch now," said David. "Or we can buy chips and Coke."

"Chips and Coke!" cried Anda, to whom chips were a novelty. Junk food, her mum would have said. You aren't having that! So, while in London she would stuff and stuff herself with junk food, Anda thought wickedly.

David looked disappointed.

"We'll cook tomorrow then," he said. "I'm a brilliant cook. I can make fantastic curries. Mum goes mad about the mess. I might be a chef when I leave school and she hates that idea!"

So they bought chips and sat in the garden eating them. Moira's garden consisted of a neatly mown, walled-in square with rose bushes. Dead boring, Anda thought. Not a weed or an insect to be seen.

"You should see our place," she said, smothering her chips with salt. "We've got some land. And goats.

"Yuk. Smelly things, goats." David made a face.

"They aren't. I'll bet you've never even seen one! Leave alone actually milked one."

"Yuk." David pretended to be sick. "Leave it out! The animal kingdom isn't really my thing. In fact I find animals positively disgusting!"

"How sad! You're really missing out. I *love* animals," said Anda seriously.

"I'd rather have a computer and a bike any day than a few musty old chickens and goats. They *pong* to high heaven."

"You can get very lonely," said Anda, "if you haven't got anything to love."

"Love!" snorted David. "I don't need *that*. You're really quaint, Anda, the way you think. I mean, well, look at my mum and dad. Said they loved each other and then Dad left, or Mum kicked him out. Mum likes to show me off to her friends. 'My son,' she calls me. 'My son this and my son that.' But *love?* No thanks."

"I've got a friend whose Mum is like that," said Anda, thinking of Julienne. "She pushed Julienne into gymnastics for her own personal glory. And Julienne cracked up. I think it taught her mum a lesson."

"Maybe I should crack up!" David said with a laugh.

"Why? Does Moira *make* you go to Sports Acrobatics?"

"No. I like it. She couldn't make me. What gets up my nose is that she uses me as an ego trip but never seems to have time to talk to me properly."

"Never mind," said Anda, sensing his resentment. She decided to change the subject. "Let's go and see the canal. Are there any boats?"

"There are, further down — there's a place where you can hire rowing boats." David cheered up immediately. He screwed up his chip paper and chucked it in the bin. "Let's go then!"

Down the road they ran, feet ringing on the pavement. Anda knew she should have changed out of her purple track suit, but she didn't care. Serve Ian Barst right if she looked tatty. She hated him! Her new trainers would get ruined too, she thought rebelliously. She had a sudden rush of glorious freedom in her head. I can do as I like in London, she thought, refusing to think about the sacrifices her parents had made to get her decent gym clothes.

Hot sun beat down, gleaming up from the railway and shimmering on grey rooftops.

Anda paused at the top of the footbridge. Strips of washing brightened a hundred gardens alongside the railway. Coppery clouds piled up behind the office building she'd named the Waffle.

"It's going to thunder!" she called to David.

"How do you know?"

"I know. I'm a country girl!"

She ran after him, feeling wild and free.

"Hey, David, see that girder down there!" she cried. "I'll bet you wouldn't dare run across it."

"I wouldn't *walk* across it. Don't be stupid, Anda!"

He stopped dead and she walked into him. They started pushing each other and from that moment, the afternoon was a riot. They mucked about and dared each other. But David refused to try the girder.

"You want your head read. Just don't try it, Anda," he warned.

"Why not? I can handle beam work. I'll bet I could do a walk over on that!"

David frowned.

"You couldn't even get up on it. Anyway you'd get disorientated up there. It's at least three metres over the water. OK if you like swimming in a yukky canal!"

"I wouldn't fall."

"But if you did? You could lay yourself out."

Anda's eyes danced.

"I'll bet you I could."

But David wouldn't rise to the dare.

"See that factory there?" he said. "That's pumping no end of gunge into the canal. You'd be seriously hurt, or poisoned, or drowned. The police are really on the ball round here. So I'm warning you. Don't!"

Anda sighed.

"All my life I've been haunted by spoilsports," she said. "People trying to stop me having fun."

"You'll have to be a stuntwoman if you feel like that," said David. He couldn't help admiring her daredevil attitude.

Before he could warn her further, Anda was gone — running like a gazelle towards a large willow tree.

"Let's climb this!"

The tree, with gnarled old branches, grew out across the canal. To David's amazement, Anda climbed expertly and swiftly to the top. He climbed after her.

"This is brilliant," he shouted. "I've never done this before. Hey! Watch your track suit on that branch!"

Suddenly Anda was caught on a broken branch which jammed itself up inside the back of her jacket.

"You look like a hunch-back!"

"A hunch-back up a tree!"

They started giggling. At the back of her mind Anda knew she was being wild and careless, just as she used to be before she became a strictly disciplined gymnast. But she didn't care. It was Ian Barst's fault, and Moira's for being stuffy. She was having a great time!

"Can't you unhook me, David? I'm stuck."

"No. I think I'll leave you there!" said David mischievously.

"You rotten swine."

The only thing to do was to slip her arms out of her jacket.

"Help me! I'm falling off the branch!" she shouted, seeing the murky canal water below her. It wasn't clean and clear like the Hooty Stream at home, but full of old tins and slime. "I can't swim very well!"

David unhooked her jacket. He held it out to her and then snatched it away again.

"Give it to me!"

"Shan't."

"Oh, *no!*" cried Anda. She looked down, and there was her purple jacket slowly sinking below the surface of the water. "Get it!" she screamed. "Lynne'll kill me if I lose it!"

David reacted swiftly. He shinned down the tree and found a long stick. He reached out and tried to hook the jacket.

"Please get it!" Anda slid down after him, barely noticing the green tree stains and pulled threads in her track suit trousers.

"I can't reach it!" said David. He shrugged and gave up. Now the jacket was completely submerged.

"Please, please," said Anda again.

"I've got tons of track suit tops. You can have one of mine. Two if you like."

"No, no. You must get it. It's my Ferndale one. Lynne and Bill sold the goats to get that for me. I've got to get it back, David. You don't understand!" howled Anda.

"Oh don't cry, Anda!"

But she couldn't help it. At home she rarely cried, and yet here she was, hysterical for the second time in one day!

"OK! I'll try again," said David. "It's not deep at the end here. Look, if I hold you, and you hold the stick, we can do it. Don't worry, we can bung it in the automatic when we get home!"

"Don't you dare let go of me," said Anda. "I can't swim very well."

"Really truly?"

"Really truly."

"You should learn!" said David. He gripped

her wrist with strong fingers and threw his weight backwards while she reached out precariously with the stick. And meanwhile the sky was growing dark as denim, and flashes of lightning lit up the buildings.

At last Anda managed to hook her dripping jacket on the end of the stick. But she couldn't pull it towards the bank.

"I'll do it. Give it here," said David.

He let go and grabbed the end of the stick. Anda almost fell in the water herself. One foot went in, up to her ankle in smelly mud. Suck, out it came, brown and gleaming. Mud oozed into her socks.

"Quick, run," shouted David. "It's going to chuck it down with rain."

Huge drops spattered them. Rolling her wet jacket into a ball, Anda followed David towards the bridge. Under the steps they sheltered.

"It stinks," said Anda, smelling her rolled-up jacket.

"Yuk," said David.

She showed him her mud-covered shoe.

"What on earth am I going to do?"

"I don't know. Rinse it in a puddle?"

That started them laughing again. They didn't dare look at each other, squashed under the sooty bridge with several other people. The rain didn't stop. On and on it pelted, scouring out the streets of London like a silver broomstick.

The enormity of what she had done to her best track suit began to dawn on Anda. The trousers were a mass of pulled threads and green tree stains. It would never be the same again. Horrified, she remembered the day Lynne had laid it out on the bed, brand new, as a surprise. Her parents had little money, and new clothes were a rarity. Always jumble sale stuff, or the Oxfam shop. Now she had ruined her lovely track suit in one hour of madness!

"It'll stop soon," said David.

He wasn't thinking about the track suit. Clothes were nothing to him. He was thinking that Anda was the greatest girl he'd ever known. You never knew what she was going to do next! David always lived a very sheltered life. Moira had never allowed him to climb trees or run wild. But in Anda's company he'd found his freedom too!

"You'll be all right, two of you together," Moira had said. "I don't mind where you go, within reason."

Anda looked at his shining eyes. She'd have to pretend the track suit didn't matter. David wouldn't like her if she fussed. So she kept quiet.

When the rain stopped they followed the towpath to the lock and watched the boats. Anda did rinse her shoe in a puddle.

"You're mad. Really mad!" said David.

"It's wet anyway. So at least it'll wash some of the mud off!"

"You'd better watch Mum's carpet when you get in. One spot of mud and she'll have apoplexy."

They hurried home in time to wash the track suit before Moira returned from work. Anda sat on the steps and peeled off her mud-soaked shoes and socks. Then she hopped upstairs on her clean foot and stuck the other one straight in the bath.

David took her track suit and socks and stuck them in the automatic. He set the switches efficiently.

"There you are. It'll be good as new!" he cried.

They were settling down to buns and television when Moira walked in.

"Hello. How did the gym go, Anda?"

"Terrible."

"You don't ask," said David.

"Oh dear." Moira put down her shopping with a clank. "What are you washing, David?"

"Only Anda's track suit. It just needed freshening up."

"Yes. Yes it did," agreed Anda, not daring to look at David.

"You've got it set far too hot!" shrieked Moira. "Haven't you got any sense, the two of you? You'll ruin it!"

Anda's heart sank. And still she had to face Ian Barst in the morning! What *would* she say to him?

"Well it's too late now," said Moira.

She disappeared upstairs.

"Oh!" Another shriek. "Who has been in this *bath?* It's got a muddy footprint!"

Anda and David looked at each other.

"I can't do a thing right. I really can't," whispered Anda.

4

He's Just Not Human!

Ian Barst looked Anda up and down critically.

"You look like something out of Oxfam."

The corner of his mouth twitched. Anda stood there, embarrassed.

"Hasn't David's mum got an iron?" Ian Barst's smile chickened out and returned to base.

"I couldn't help it. David — I — we dropped it in the canal and then we washed it too hot." Anda lifted her chin defiantly. "And I haven't got another. We haven't got pots of money. So tough cookies."

David winced. Anda really was pushing her luck.

But Ian Barst's smile finally made it. Crack. Like an old conker splitting.

"I like a bit of fire!" he said. "Makes a good gymnast. Frankly, Anda, I'm surprised you had the guts to come back here."

Anda twisted away from his friendly pat and stared at him stonily.

David escorted her to the warm-up room.

"My cousin," he said to everyone they met. He seemed proud of her now. But only because she'd been lippy to Ian Barst, Anda thought, not because of her skill as a gymnast.

After warm-up Ian Barst was waiting.

"Let's tackle your tumbling runs first." He waved her towards a matted area. "Show me the first one you did yesterday."

That was a round off, two back flips, a back somersault and a back walkover to stag sit. Easy. Anda threw herself into it. Of course it went wrong. She bungled the back somie and landed on her bottom. Infuriating! A rare occurrence, but it had to happen in front of Ian Barst!

"Try again."

She did. Half-heartedly.

"Height, height, height!" Ian Barst was shouting. "And again."

Again she tried, putting extra effort into it.

"No, no, *no!*"

"I really can't go any higher!" she said.

"You can. You aren't using half the power you've got! Feet and ankles. That's your trouble. Do some ankle exercises. Every night and morning. Six times a day. And listen to what I'm telling you."

Height was Anda's strong point. Or so she'd thought! Obediently she listened to Ian Barst. He used long words and phrases unfamiliar to her, like hyper-extension and kinesthetic awareness. Not wanting to appear thick, she pretended to understand. And that was a recipe for disaster!

"You haven't listened to a thing I've said!" he raved.

And so it went on. Shout, shout, shout. Until in desperation Anda *did* begin to think about what he was saying. But by the time she'd understood what he wanted she was too exhausted to carry it out, and only anger kept her going. She got sick of doing the same tumbling run and wished she could go on the bars or the beam.

Her head rang, her throat wanted to cry and her limbs felt like melted jelly.

"OK. Stop."

"I was just beginning to understand!" said Anda angrily.

"That's the time to stop, then. You'll do it tomorrow."

"I shan't. I can't do it the way you want it."

"I'd like to see you vault in a minute." He ignored her depressed look. "You go and warm up on the vault. Carol will spot you. I'll be there in about ten minutes."

"Right, now I'll show him," Anda thought, heading for the vaulting room.

Nell was there, doing Yamashita vaults with a very red face. She was good at them. Run, whip, flick, over she went, thin as a swallow. Secretly Anda felt sure *she* could do a Yamashita vault, but she hadn't been allowed to try yet.

She was surprised to see Carol there in a track suit.

"I'm training to be a coach," she explained. "Otherwise I'll have had it when I'm eighteen. I don't want some nice office job after this! You ready to vault then?"

"Yes." Anda rubbed her hands on the faded

training tights that Julienne had given her.

"What vault are you doing?"

Anda didn't know what made her say it. Silly pride? A wish to impress Carol? Or reluctance to admit she, Anda Barnes, winner of the coveted scholarship, had not progressed to Nell's standard!

"Yammies," she said arrogantly.

Carol raised an eyebrow.

"What — straight away?"

"No — I'll do a couple of handspring vaults first."

"Ian likes you to do all your vaults first."

"I've only got ten minutes," explained Anda, "so I won't."

"Whatever you say!"

Obviously Carol was not happy about it. She seemed nervous about spotting, and that didn't improve Anda's confidence. Already her heart was thudding as she did her handspring vaults. But she was too hyped-up to consider backing out of the Yamashita.

"Right — a Yammy this time!" she called, and Carol nodded.

Anda considered what a Yammy involved. Then she threw herself towards the springboard. Bang! Up into a handstand. She whipped her legs up ready for the pike shape she was supposed to make in the air. Inevitably she fell backwards. Carol cried out, lunged forward to catch Anda and they both fell crash against the vaulting horse.

Anda gasped and clutched her face, which she had banged on the corner of the horse. Shocked, she looked up at Carol, who was standing over her using the foulest language.

"I've broken my jaw!" howled Anda, panicking. Feeling sick with the pain, she staggered to the wall and curled up against it.

Carol was clutching her stomach.

"That's nothing. You've split me!"

Anda took deep breaths. Lynne had taught her that. It stops you hurting, and it stops you crying, she'd said.

"What on earth were you trying to do, you irresponsible idiot!" Carol didn't care about Anda's jaw. "You shouldn't even be doing Yammies!" She stood over Anda, rubbing her side angrily. "That's the last time I'm spotting *you!*"

"Leave it out, Carol!"

To Anda's surprise, the kind arm round her shoulders was Nell's arm. The pain in her cheek was monstrous. She didn't dare speak, or remove her hand to inspect the damage. Words queued in her throat. I wish I'd never come here. I'm not responsible. I'm not. But she couldn't say them.

"I'll be OK in a minute," she gasped.

"It's probably a bruise," said Nell kindly. "Shall I get Brenda?"

"No one cares how many ribs I've broken," said Carol.

Anda shook her head. Of course she hadn't broken her jaw! And Carol hadn't broken any ribs.

She stood up, slowly. Her left cheek was red and swelling.

"Sorry," she said to Carol. "I made a mess of it."

"Have you actually done a Yamashita vault before?" demanded Carol.

Anda was silent.

"Well, have you?"

"No."

She thought Carol would hit the ceiling.

"Please, please don't tell Ian," begged Anda when Carol had finished swearing at her.

"Your language, Carol!" reproved Nell.

"It's none of your business, Nell."

Anda rubbed her throbbing face.

"Please don't!" she pleaded, seeing Ian Barst approaching.

"All right." Carol sighed. "I guess I did everything wrong, too, when I came here. We'll forget it."

Thank goodness Carol was human!

But Ian Barst wasn't. If he noticed Anda's ripening bruise he didn't comment.

"Are we going to stand around all day or are we going to vault?"

The six longed-for weeks of training stretched bleakly ahead in Anda's mind. Not only that, she had to survive Moira and London. And wearing a crumpled purple track suit every day.

When Ian Barst asked her about her vault she had the sense to say, "Just a handspring."

It didn't make much difference anyway. She felt so down. Gamely she waited at the end of the run-up carpet.

"I don't need spotting for this one," she called.

But he stood there anyway. A spark of confidence came. At least Ian Barst could catch her. She'd watched him, deft and strong, spotting Nell and Keewong.

She aimed and ran, swiftly, then lengthening her stride to time her take-off. It's a good one! she thought as her feet left the reuther-board. Her flight was good, her landing square and steady. A winner, she thought, and Ian Barst's raised eyebrows confirmed it.

Feeling better, she ran back for a second attempt. Her face ached but she didn't care. The speed and daring flight of vaulting never failed to inspire her. If I wasn't human, she'd said once to Julienne, I'd be a bird, a truly aerobatic bird!

After her second go at the handspring vault, Ian Barst stopped her.

"You're arching your back a little bit too much, and your angle of take-off is wrong..." He launched into a complicated set of instructions.

Another gruelling, repetitive session followed. Again and again Anda did her handspring vault, trying to adjust it the way he wanted. Exhaustion loomed. Her face, hands and feet burned and everything in between felt weak. The session ended in a surprising way.

"Quite apart from anything else, you aren't fit. You're too fat," declared Ian Barst after another set of instructions. "I shall have to put you on a diet."

Too fat! Me! Anda was speechless. Then furious. No one had ever said such a thing to her. Of course I'm not fat, she thought, incensed. She glimpsed Ian Barst laughing with Carol.

That did it!

She tore down the run-up carpet like a furious terrier. Pounce. Bang. Whip.

"Hooray!"

Carol and Ian Barst were actually cheering.

"Well done! That was ten score perfect!" cried Ian Barst.

Anda smiled widely, happily. All the morning's torture was cancelled out by that one compliment.

"It works every time!" Ian Barst joked to Carol. "Tell 'em they're too fat and they'll do a ten score vault out of sheer rage!"

"You did it to me!" agreed Carol. "Well done, Anda."

"Stop at that." Ian Barst waved his arm towards the canteen, where David was hovering in the doorway. "You go and have a break now, Anda. Then Carol will show you some new exercises I want you to practise."

Anda pulled on her track suit gratefully.

"I think," Ian Barst wagged a finger at her, "I might be able to do something with you after all. No pigging cream cakes in there! Keep her on the lemon juice, Nell."

Nell went with her to the canteen.

"I want to meet your cousin," she said. "I really fancy him!"

"What, David?" cried Anda in disbelief. "How can you fancy him?"

"I think he's fab. You want to see him working," enthused Nell.

"I don't think he's good-looking," said Anda.

"But he can be a laugh. He's mad!"

She'd forgotten her money, so David bought her a strawberry milk shake.

"I'll pay you back," she said. "I'm not used to carrying money — I never need it at home."

Wistfully she sat remembering her own dear Ferndale Gym Club, in that lovely lawned house with its dark cedar trees. And Christie and John who had proudly coaxed her into being the gymnast she was. Then she thought of the Hooty Stream tinkling past their cottage, and Bella her cat chasing leaves in the sun. And here she was in roaring London, her track suit ruined, her confidence in tatters, and the precious training grant fast disappearing on Tube fares and cans of Coke! Don't you *dare* fritter it away on junk food and silly souvenirs, Lynne had warned. One pound-fifty was gone already, then she must repay David. Two pounds. A pound a day! Seven pounds a week. Six sevens are —

"What are you doing, Anda?" David came into focus. "Adding something up?"

"Yes." She was back in the present. "Ian Barst said I was too fat!"

"Oh Anda!" cried Nell.

"That's *ridiculous!*" snorted David.

"He says that to everyone," advised another girl who was drinking Coke at a nearby table.

Anda patted her stomach thoughtfully.

"I don't see how I can be. Lynne's always nagging me to eat!"

She gazed out into the gym which suddenly looked full of pin-thin brilliant gymnasts. None of them had tatty track suits. Anda wished her best friend Julienne was there. Julienne was kind and understanding. She would have turned out her wardrobe, offering Anda "this old thing" or "that old thing I never wear".

"She's gone again!" teased Nell, making eyes at David. "Dreaming about that country cottage, are you?"

"No," said Anda. "But I'll have to go on a diet. I'll be too broke to eat anyway."

She looked longingly at David's salad roll.

"We'll raid the cupboard tomorrow and bring sandwiches," he said.

"Then I'll get fat!" said Anda, and they all laughed.

Oddly she began to feel part of things. She liked Nell, who reminded her of Kerry, a girl at Ferndale Gym Club. She liked Carol too, since she'd kept quiet about the disastrous Yammy. A hard session with Ian Barst seemed to breed friendship among the girls. They'd all been through it.

"All I did was one lousy tumbling run and one vault for the whole morning!" she moaned to David on the way home.

"You did all right, Anda. Stop worrying!"

Outside the Tube station was a greengrocer's. David marched into it.

"Wait there!"

He reappeared with a lettuce.

"Present for you. Diet?"

Anda stared at his mischievous face.

"You rat!"

She threw the lettuce at him. He threw it back, harder. Laughing, they ran down the street, with the lettuce going to and fro.

I'm not me. I'm not being myself at all, said a little voice in Anda's mind. Mum would go potty about me wasting one of God's lettuces.

Moira was heaving some shopping up the steps when they reached home.

"Anda! You look terrible! What happened to your face?"

"It's an occupational hazard," said David.

"And your track suit! It looks awful! Whatever will Lynne say? And Bill? Didn't he sell his precious goat to get that for you?"

Concerned, but tactless, Moira stood like a schoolteacher awaiting an answer.

A picture of her dad loomed in Anda's mind. She saw clearly his kind, merry face, and remembered his lovely philosophy that didn't rate clothes and possessions above people's feelings. She could almost have touched him, the vision was so real. For the first time in her life she could not throw herself against his denim jacket and howl out her troubles.

"I wish — I wish Dad were here," she choked.

"Well, ring him up," said Moira brightly.

"No." Anda shook her head. "The phone isn't any good. I need to see him. I..."

Obviously David and Moira wouldn't understand. Anda fled upstairs and locked herself in the bathroom.

Silently she gazed at her crumpled, bruised reflection.

I'd better not cry, she thought, fighting back the hot flood of tears. I've done nothing but cry since I came to London.

5

Homesick

David glared at Moira. "I won't be seen with you!" he hissed. "Mums don't jog!"

"They can if they want to." Anda stuck up for Moira. Jogging before breakfast was part of Anda's new fitness scheme and Moira, who wanted to lose weight, had decided to join in.

David left the house ahead of them. Anda could have caught up with him, but she decided to stay with Moira. This morning Anda was glad to run slowly. She had a nagging gut ache. Ignoring it didn't work. It had been there at bedtime, and was still there when she woke up in the morning. She was afraid to tell Moira. She was afraid of being sent to the doctor and told she had appendicitis. It was something Anda dreaded.

"This isn't going to last!" Moira gasped as they reached the towpath.

"See that girder?" said Anda. "I'd really like to dance on that!"

"Don't you ever *dare!*" cried Moira in horror.

"I want to be a stuntwoman when I leave school."

Two weeks had passed. Hard weeks of gruelling training sessions with Ian Barst, sweltering journeys in the Tube, and long afternoons messing about with David. No rain had fallen, and London resembled an oven, its glass door closed and smoke-stained. Anda longed to go home for a weekend, but it would cost too much money. She'd agreed to stick it out.

Twice a week, Bill and Lynne rang her from Gran's house.

"I'm OK," she always said. "Yes, the training's going fine. Yes, I get on all right with David. Yes, Moira's looking after me. No, I'm not living on junk food."

She played it really cool, pretending there was nothing to fuss about. But Bill knew.

"Something's wrong!" he frowned as he replaced the phone after his Tuesday call to Anda.

"What do you mean? Wrong?" asked Lynne.

"Nonsense," said Gran briskly. "She's quite all right! Spoke to her myself only on Friday. She said she'd been doing a back somersault dismount from the high bars. She sounded pleased about that!"

"No," said Bill determinedly. "I know Anda. There's something wrong. She's telling us the good bits to stop us fussing."

"Well what can be wrong? Could she be homesick? She wouldn't say so!" worried Lynne.

"Homesick. Nonsense. She'll have to get over that," said Gran. "When I was a girl I..."

"No. It's something else," insisted Bill. "She might be homesick but she'd weather that. It's maybe that she's worried about her training and can't talk to anyone. Or maybe Moira is..."

"Bill," said Gran sharply.

"Or that David."

"Anda likes David. She was telling me what fun they were having," said Gran.

"Should we go up? said Lynne. "She'll think we're fussing."

"If she's miserable she's coming home. Like it or not. I'll fetch her myself," threatened Bill.

"Wait until we ring up on Friday," said Lynne. "Then we'll have a go at her. She can't waste her summer holiday up there being miserable."

Lynne worried herself into a state of hysteria on the way back to Hooty Cottage. Bill was cross with her.

"For goodness' sake, Lynne! I wish I'd never said anything now!"

But Lynne went on and on.

"You don't know *who* David is mixed up with. They're left on their own every afternoon while Moira's at work. Supposing she's got mixed up with glue sniffers or something? We'd never forgive ourselves, Bill!"

Anda put the phone down, feeling desperate. David had gone off to his Karate club and Moira was watching television.

Anda looked at the phone. Maybe she could

phone Gran again? Bill would have gone and Gran would only tell her to pull herself together. Nell and Carol lived far away, and anyway she didn't have their phone numbers. Of course, Julienne! It was Julienne she needed to talk to. Julienne was a mine of information. She would know the answer to the question that was bugging Anda!

Eagerly she dialled Julienne's number. But the phone rang and rang in the empty flat. Anda walked upstairs heavily, and checked the dates on the letter Julienne had written her. Julienne was on holiday in Wales that week.

"Why do I feel so ill?" Anda asked her reflection in the mirror. Her stomach hurt, a low heavy pain that she'd never had before.

"I've got appendicitis. I know I have!" she cried to herself, and rolled on the bed, clutching her stomach.

In a panic she crawled to the bathroom and made herself a hot-water bottle. She didn't dare tell Moira. Or David. They would call the doctor and she would be sent to hospital for an operation. Anda was terrified of hospitals. And what if she had surgery? She'd never work on the bars again!

Thinking about it made her feel sick. She curled up under the quilt, still with her shoes on, and fell into a deep sleep.

"Brenda," she thought as she dozed off. "I'll talk to Brenda at the gym club in the morning."

When she awoke, Moira was standing over her.

"Don't you want your supper, Anda? It's

eight o'clock.

Anda sat up, embarrassed. She'd been asleep for two hours! The pain was still there.

"Oh no!" she groaned.

"Whatever's the matter?" Moira peered at her. "You look quite pale. Come to think of it, you look pretty dreadful."

"Nothing! I don't look pale. It's just the light." Anda got up quickly.

"I wish you wouldn't lie on the bed with your shoes on! Are you sure you're all right?"

"Yes. I'm fine," lied Anda. "But I don't really fancy any supper."

The smell of curry cooking turned her stomach.

"You can have bangers if you don't want curry," said Moira.

"No thanks. Really. I'm OK." She wished Moira would go away.

"You can't not eat! I know you're on a diet, Anda, but this is ridiculous. Shall I make you a cheese omelette?"

"No, really. I've got a tummy bug, I expect."

Of course that was the wrong thing to say to Moira!

"A tummy bug? Oh no, that's all we need. I'll have to disinfect the bathroom. And mind you wash your hands. I must remind David to wash his! Are you sure that's what you've got?"

Anda shrugged desolately. Lynne would have given her a hug and not hassled her. But Moira persisted.

"You're nearly crying, Anda!" She sat down on the bed. "What's wrong? You can tell me!"

"I've got gut ache," said Anda stonily, holding on to her tears. "There's no need to fuss."

"All right." Moira stood up again. She liked Anda and felt slightly hurt that Anda wouldn't confide in her. "If you aren't better in the morning, I'm ringing the doctor. At least come downstairs and have a cup of cocoa or something."

David appeared in the doorway.

"See if you can do something with her," hissed Moira. "And for goodness' sake wash your hands, David. She's got a tummy bug or something."

"Hi!" said Anda. David was the last person she needed. But at least he wouldn't hassle her.

"Come on, Anda! Don't you want to watch 'Fame'?"

"Oh, all right. It'll take my mind off this gut ache."

She paused at the landing window. London was bathed in golden sunset light. The Waffle's windows blazed and the railway glinted. Anda longed to be sitting in her favourite birch tree by the Hooty Stream, watching the seagulls winging their way home and the rabbits coming out to play as darkness fell. How can I bear it? she thought. For four more weeks!

"Come on, Anda, it's started!" David had already collapsed into an armchair with a huge plate of curry.

"I — need to make a phone call first."

Suddenly, without asking Moira, Anda was dialling Gran's number, her heart aching.

"Hello Gran," she said in barely a whisper. "It's me, Anda."

"Oh, hello again dear!" Gran sounded surprised. Anda pictured her concerned eyes, and suddenly she couldn't speak.

"Is something wrong, dear?"

"No," she choked.

"You're crying, Anda! What is it dear?"

Silence. Gran tried again.

"Get a hold on yourself dear. Take some deep breaths. Now you tell Gran."

But Anda couldn't. Life was so simple for Gran, she thought. How could Gran understand?

"I really need to talk to Mum or Dad," she managed to say.

"What is it, love? Do you need money?"

"Well..." Anda hesitated. "Yes I do — but there's something else. It's really bugging me and I need to talk to Mum, or — even Julienne, except that she's on holiday."

"Can't you tell Moira?"

"No."

"Why ever not?"

"She's — well — it's difficult."

"Can it wait until the morning, dear? I really don't want to get the car out and drive all the way up to Hooty Cottage now. It's nearly dark."

Gran hated driving in the dark! Anda sighed.

"Sorry. OK Gran, it'll have to wait. Never mind."

"Well, you can tell me. Are you ill? Are you in trouble?"

"No — no. Don't worry, Gran. Really."

"But..."

"I'll have to go now. Moira's phone bill!"

"Why didn't you say there was something wrong earlier on?"

Anda turned to see Moira listening in the kitchen doorway. Eavesdropping! Anda glared.

"You could have told me!" Moira looked hurt. "Is that Mum you're talking to? Let me have a word with her."

"She's just ringing off," said Anda. But Moira took the phone from her.

"Oh dear!" Anda walked into the lounge and sat down, kicking the chair moodily. "That's done it!"

"What's the matter?" asked David.

"Oh I rang Gran because I wanted to have a moan to Dad, and now she'll tell Moira and there'll be an awful fuss!"

"Well you shouldn't have rung her."

"You're a big help."

"Come on. Have some supper. It's curry!"

"No thanks."

Anda tried to watch "Fame", but bright television and noise made her feel worse. Back came the pain! Appendicitis, she thought, terrified. She muttered something about going to bed early, and returned to her room.

"Don't come up," she told Moira. "I'll be all right. I only want some sleep."

Sleep proved impossible. She tossed and turned while the orange lights of London glimmered across the ceiling. Trains pounded and faded. David and Moira argued downstairs. She heard David come to bed and kick his shoes off. Clump. Clump. Then Moira's bath running, the hairdryer whirring. Then drunks going home from the pub.

And finally London's attempt at silence.

Anda imagined Hooty Cottage at night. Through the window she tried to see the stars beyond the orange street lamps. Those same stars shone on Hooty Cottage. Seeing them brought home closer. She could almost hear the owls and the wind.

In the morning, she thought, I'll go early and ask Brenda about this stomach ache.

Eventually she slept. And slept!

David went to the gym club without her.

"Leave her," Moira said. "And here's a note for Ian Barst. Anda's in for a surprise this morning!"

At last the sound of rattling taxis, trains and buses penetrated Anda's sleep. Morning rush hour!

Horrified, she stared at her travelling clock. Ten o'clock. Ian Barst would go mad! And she wouldn't be able to see Brenda.

As she swung her legs out of bed, she heard an unbelievable sound downstairs. A voice. Her Bill's voice, talking to Moira. Then his long legs were running up the stairs. The door opened, and there he was!

"Bill!" she screamed. "How did you get here?"

"I left at five o'clock this morning. Gran came up, after your phone call. She was beside herself with worry."

"Oh Bill! I'm so pleased to see you." Anda clung to him, glad to feel his denim jacket and bristly beard. He smelled of the greenhouse. "You've been tying up tomatoes!" she laughed. "Pong!"

"I've come to take you home." Bill was in no mood for chatter.

Slowly the words sank in.

"Oh, no! No, Bill!" Anda backed away. "You can't do that! You can't!"

"Can't I!"

She stared at Bill's eyes. He wasn't joking.

Odd how the thing she'd most wanted seemed totally wrong when she faced it. She *didn't* want to go home. She wanted to go on training! Even with Ian Barst. She was going to be a champion like Carol. And that meant dedication.

And survival!

Half an hour of hard talking convinced Bill. Lynne would have insisted. But Bill, wisely, didn't.

"All right, Anda," he said finally. "If you must do it, you must. I can't influence you. But you've got to stop this dieting nonsense! Lynne would go spare if she saw the way you look. You look positively anorexic!"

"It isn't that I'm dieting really," Anda explained.

"Moira's food is so weird, and I have this rotten gut ache, but I don't want Moira to take me to the doctor. I won't go. She can drag me, and I won't go."

"Whereabouts is your gut ache?" Again Bill had the sense not to insist.

"Here." Anda pointed vaguely. "I expect it's just a bug."

Bill took her shoulders.

"Look at me Anda."

She tried, and couldn't.

"What are you scared of?"

Two tears rolled down her cheeks.

"Appendicitis."

"Most unlikely," said Bill reassuringly. "Didn't we have this scare at home once and the doctor said it was nerves? I'm sure if you have a good meal and a bit of a kip you'll be fine."

But privately he was worried. He resolved to get Anda to the doctor, or the doctor to Anda, somehow! He wished Lynne had come instead of him.

"I really need to see Julienne," Anda said. "I wish she could come up."

"Well perhaps she can. She was saying how much she envied you. I expect Moira would put her up for a week if it would help you survive. You've got two beds in here."

Anda brightened.

"Oh, could she? That would be brilliant! She could come to the gym club and watch. She'd love it. Oh do try and arrange it! She'll be home from Wales on Saturday!"

"Perhaps she could come up on Sunday then?"

"That's only four days away!"

Anda couldn't wait.

But she could not have forseen what a disastrous effect Julienne's visit was to have!

6

It's Impossible

CRASH! Anda fell three metres from the top bar. For the umpteenth time that morning she crashed into the foam pit. The novelty had worn off and now every bone in her body ached as she tried to learn an eagle catch on the high bar. Every time she managed the wrap with enough speed, she couldn't get the grip right.

"Drive your hips against the bar," Ian Barst kept shouting.

"Maybe I'm just too small." Anda climbed out of the foam pit yet again. Although the bars were adjustable, Anda frequently envied the taller girls with their long arms. It looked easier for them.

"That's a negative attitude," said Ian Barst sternly. "You think positive. OK you're small — so you've got to fly farther, stretch harder, swing faster. So in the end you'll be a better gymnast than a taller girl. Look at these Russian girls! The little ones score every time."

"But they have to work twice as hard!"

moaned Anda, and privately she wondered what became of those tiny girls who performed so brilliantly. What kind of lives did they have when they were no longer in the limelight?

It was the wrong thing to say to Ian Barst. He wouldn't tolerate moaning. David had told him Anda wasn't well, but he'd ignored that, and she hadn't yet had the chance to see Brenda.

She swung herself up again, aware of a gripping pain in her stomach and a sense of despair.

Carol was spotting her. Anda whipped herself around the lower bar, and stopped.

"Not enough speed," said Carol.

Anda took a deep breath and tried again. She managed the wrap around, and the swift back stretch into the eagle shape. But again her hands failed her. CRASH.

"I just don't have the strength in my hands to grip in that position. It's impossible!" she sighed.

At least Carol was kinder than Ian.

"I felt like that when I was learning. Don't worry. You're doing all right."

After another gruelling twenty minutes with no success, Anda was shattered, mentally and physically.

"I'll *never* do an eagle," she wept to Nell during a break. Tears *again*, she thought, ashamed. But that was gymnastics. Poetry and pain, flying and falling. Why was she so hooked on it? "I feel like an old woman," she said, trying to sip milk between sobs.

"I know what you mean." Nell was

sympathetic. "Us gymnasts have to grow up quicker. Never mind," she added brightly, "the rest of life will be a doddle after this!"

"My dad drove up to see me yesterday," said Anda. "He was so worried about me. He left Mum to cope with all the animals..."

But Nell wasn't listening. She was too busy watching David training on the pommel horse.

"I need to see Brenda." Anda gulped the rest of her milk.

But before she could find Brenda she went to the loo and made a horrific discovery. She was bleeding!

"Oh no! No. No!" she cried, and went cold from top to toe. Was it the curse? The first time ever! Or was it some terrible internal injury by slamming against the bars?

In a cold sweat she unbolted the door and staggered to the bench against the wall. A girl she didn't know was there, washing her hands.

"Can you get Brenda?" gasped Anda. "I'm dying."

The girl gave her a wild look.

"I'll get Brenda! Lie down or something."

Anda curled over on the bench, her cheek against the cool tiled wall. Melodrama was not her usual style. She was genuinely scared.

Brenda soon sorted her out. She appeared at speed, First Aid bag over her shoulder. Her presence was reassuring.

"Whatever's the matter, Anda?"

Anda froze. Though she wanted Brenda, she found it impossible to say what was wrong.

"Come on. Take your hands away from your

face," persuaded Brenda, and she turned to the concerned onlookers who had gathered. "And you lot. Out! None of your business!"

The girls disappeared. No one crossed Brenda! But Nell hovered. And David, a respectable distance from the loo door, hovered too.

"Why didn't you say something was wrong?" asked Nell.

"Go on, Nell. I'll deal with it," insisted Brenda, sensing Anda's embarrassment.

Nell went reluctantly.

"Now you tell Brenda. Are you hurt? Have you got a tummy ache?"

Somehow Brenda had a way of making it all right to behave like a two-year-old.

Anda nodded.

"Stomach ache. I've had it for days and now I'm bleeding," she burst out letting go of her panic. "And now I don't know whether it's *that* — you know — or whether I've got internal injuries from all the bar work — or a burst appendix — I know someone who had one..."

Brenda was reassuring. After a brief interrogation and a few prods at Anda's tummy she knew the cause.

"It's the curse. That's all. Nothing to worry about. Haven't you had it before?"

"No."

"You do know what it is?"

"Of course I do," said Anda, cross with herself. "Mum's told me lots of times, and Julienne. If I'd known it was only that I wouldn't have worried."

Brenda wagged her finger.

"You should have asked me before. I could have told you it was probably that! Come on, we'll fix you up with something and you won't know you've got it!"

Anda suddenly felt fine again. She jumped to her feet.

"I can go on training!" she cried. "I'm learning the eagle catch."

"That's right."

"If only I'd known what it was! I couldn't possibly talk to Moira about it! I suppose I'll have to now."

"Don't worry," said Brenda. "I'll fix you up. I'll give you plenty so you won't have to go shopping this time."

"Thanks. Thanks Brenda!"

Brenda found Anda some clean clothes and she re-emerged into the gym, feeling light-headed and bouncy again. Her eyes sparkled as she ran to the bars

"Hey, are you better now?" called Nell.

"Yes thanks. It was just the curse," said Anda, with a grin.

"What was up with you?" asked David.

"Nothing," she snapped, embarrassed. She caught Nell's eyes and they giggled. "Nothing to do with you, David."

He rolled his eyes.

"Women!"

"That's about it!"

She and Nell burst out laughing and David returned to his pommel horse.

Anda worked alone on the bars, practising the

difficult hand grip. Despite her shame about making a fuss, the relief of knowing put her on an artificial high. She suppressed her uneasiness about the curse. She imagined Julienne's reaction: Oh *that!* I've had it for *years*. Julienne was coming on Sunday for a week, and after that one more week of training. Then home, and back to Ferndale for the annual Club Championship.

"I've no hope of winning it!" she told David on the way home. "This year I've got to go in the over-elevens group and they're all miles better than me. I shan't even get a medal."

"Never mind," said David. "I don't care about medals. Medals are for your mum's ego trips."

"Lynne isn't like that."

"Lucky you. Did you manage your eagle catch?"

"No," said Anda. "Not this morning. But I shall do soon. I certainly feel more optimistic about it."

"Is your friend a gymnast too? Julienne?"

"She was. I told you. She cracked up because of her pushy mother. You might have a lot in common with her."

"I doubt it. You needn't hang round me, the two of you," said David, suddenly angry. "I shall go off on my own."

"Oh David! Don't be like that!"

But David smouldered all the way home. Anda couldn't understand his attitude. Could he be jealous?

She tried to ask him but he disappeared into his room with a slam. Anda had been so preoccupied with her own problems she'd barely noticed that David's bad mood had begun when Julienne's visit was arranged.

"He'll get over it. Take no notice," said Moira that evening. "He didn't want you to come at first. Now he thinks you're great!"

"He doesn't!" said Anda in astonishment.

"He does!" said Moira. "I expect he feels threatened by Julienne. He thinks you'll be two girls together and he'll be left out."

"Oh, that's stupid! Of course he won't be." Anda was surprised at Moira's flash of insight. She looked at her quizzically. Perhaps I could have confided in her after all, she thought. Perhaps I haven't given her a chance to be human.

Moira was right. David did feel threatened by Julienne's visit. He liked Anda. She was fun to be with and he'd enjoyed their afternoons mucking about by the canal. He didn't want some giggly girlfriend monopolizing Anda. If Julienne was anything like that Nell, he thought, he'd hate her.

So on Sunday David refused to go with them to the station. He shut himself in his room with his stereo and his computer and Anda went to the club alone. Moira was to meet her there and take her to Paddington to meet Julienne's train.

Anda was better. Her appetite had returned, and she felt more like herself. She could even manage alone on the Tube. She flashed a smile at Ian Barst.

"That's better!" he said. "I can work with you if you smile!"

Perhaps I've misjudged him. He's really quite nice. Maybe I misjudged Moira too, thought Anda as she chalked her hands. I've been in such a state! She swung up on to the bars, practising underswing upstarts. She felt strong and inspired. Carol stood watching her, helping where she could.

"Can you tell Ian I'm ready to try the eagle?" Anda perched on the top bar, examining her hands. They were hard and blistered from bar work. Sometimes the blisters broke and needed dressing with some stuff that stung like fury. She swung down and chalked them again.

"You're asking for trouble with that blister," Ian Barst said, looking over her shoulder. "Wear some guards."

"I don't..."

"Wear them. Or I won't coach you."

Sighing, Anda put on her hand guards. Wretched things!

"I wish I had thick skin like a rhinoceros," she said.

Up she went, whipping herself round the bars at great speed. Crash! Into the foam pit. She'd missed the catch again! Up again, with Ian Barst's gnome-like face watching attentively.

Finally, in a thrilling moment, she managed an eagle catch. If only Christie or John could have seen her! Or Gran!

"Well done. And again. Now you're thinking!" said Ian Barst.

And when she danced into the canteen for her break, there was no one to share her euphoria!

"Oh shut up about it!" said Nell. "You wait

till he makes you do a full twisting back somie like I've been doing! I reckon I've put a bone out in my neck, and he won't take any notice."

Moira turned up late and panicking in a taxi.

"Come on quickly, Anda!" she yelled. "Paddington Station now, please."

Anda fell into the taxi.

"I did the eagle catch at last," she said as the taxi lurched off into the traffic.

"Oh really? What's that?" Without waiting for an answer, Moira started attacking Anda about her appearance. "Look at this bag, Anda. Do you have to stuff your track suit in like that with the sleeves hanging out! And must you go round in those dirty old trainers?"

Furious, Anda turned to Moira, her eyes blazing.

"I don't think that's fair," she said bluntly.

"Anda!"

Encouraged by Moira's shocked eyes, Anda decided to finish what she wanted to say. It was time someone told Moira.

"You've got your priorities scrambled," she said. "You don't care about people's feelings — only their appearance."

There was an explosive silence while the taxi weaved in and out of the traffic.

"Well! I'm sorry you think that, after all I've tried to do for you! And I'm having your friend to stay! I hope she's not like you! Anda, I'm really hurt."

"Sorry," mumbled Anda resentfully. She stared out of the window. Now she felt guilty for hurting Moira. "Julienne's not like me," she said. "She's like an angel. And she's into ballet and music and she's much more educated and articulate than me."

"Thank goodness for that!"

Excitedly Anda waited on the long platform for Julienne's train. At least Julienne would understand about the eagle catch. She couldn't wait to tell her.

At last the train came, the blue and yellow diesel whistling slowly into the platform. The doors opened and Anda stood up on a luggage trolley, looking for Julienne's brown head with its two thick plaits and friendly blue eyes.

"Get down off there!" pleaded Moira.

But Anda was not prepared for the change in her friend's image. Suddenly Julienne was there, her hair cut and permed into silky curls. She wore slick cut-off jeans and a black jacket. Only twelve, but she looked eighteen!

"You've had your hair permed!" screamed Anda.

"Yes!" The same bluebell eyes twinkled at her. "And you've got thin, Anda! Look at you!"

"I did an eagle catch this morning."

Julienne gasped. She gave Anda a hug.

"That's fantastic! It really is! Christie will freak."

"And I've started the curse!"

"Oh *that!*" said Julienne, rolling her eyes. "I've had *that* for years!"

7

Anda Is Angry

"I'm not coming down," frowned David. "I'm busy."

Surrounded by half-eaten sandwiches, Coke cans and cassettes, David lolled on his bed like an angry sultan.

"And I've had my lunch, thanks."

"You might at least come and meet Julienne!" said Anda, hurt at his behaviour.

"She's not coming in here. This room is private. And that includes you."

"All right. Be like that. See if I care."

Anda tossed her head angrily. Without another word she left David to stew. Julienne was unpacking in her bedroom.

"He's in a sulk. He can really be so childish," said Anda, flopping on her bed. The whole room felt different with Julienne in it. Better, and friendlier.

"I brought you this. Here, have it."

A purple Ferndale track suit emerged from Julienne's bag. She threw it at Anda.

Anda gave a scream of delight. On the phone she'd told Julienne about her own track suit getting ruined.

"You can't *give* it to me."

"I can. It's only an old thing. It's too tight for me now anyway!"

"It's too big for me!" cried Anda, trying it on. "But that doesn't matter."

"No. You look good in it. Elfish!" teased Julienne.

"Shut up! What about you then, with your hair permed!"

"Oh, that's Mummy. She treated me. She's been trying to stop me growing up for years and suddenly gets this thing about me looking too little-girlish."

"Maybe you did, but you look — so different now!" Anda couldn't quite get used to Julienne's bouncing curls. Critically she examined her own straggly reflection, doubtful now about the pony tail she'd taken trouble to grow. Her appearance never worried her before but now, beside Julienne, she felt like an insignificant mouse.

"Your Gran sent this for you, Anda. Not to be spent on junk food. Strict orders from Lynne!" Julienne fished in her bag and produced a five-pound note.

"I needed that! Bless Gran — she always knows what I need."

"Were you skint? London's so expensive, isn't it?"

"I was. I can pay David back for the milk shakes now," said Anda happily. Money had been another major worry. She remembered the rowing boats they hadn't been able to afford. "I know. I'll treat us to a rowing boat this afternoon. That'll put David in a good mood again. He's been really nice to me, Julienne."

After lunch, which consisted of Julienne's omelettes and salad (strict orders from Lynne), they ran upstairs and knocked on David's door.

"Now what?" David opened the door crossly.

"We're going to hire a boat. My treat!" said Anda. "And here's what I owe you for the milk shakes. And this is Julienne."

David glanced at Julienne with a surprised look in his eyes. Then he looked away again quickly. What he saw, briefly, was a decent, pretty-looking girl. Not what he'd expected at all.

"Please do come with us, David," begged Anda. "We aren't much good at rowing. We can't take a boat out without you."

David hesitated.

"Oh, all right."

"Hey, wow, you've got a computer!" said Julienne, peeping into his room. "Is it yours?"

"Yes. I don't really want it disturbed right now. I'm working on something," said David importantly. "But I've got some computer games we could play later, if you like."

Anda rolled her eyes. She'd consistently refused to get involved in David's computer games, which she disliked and didn't understand. Boring, she'd thought. But Julienne was enthusiastic.

"Yes, I'd love to!"

"Well come on — let's go and hire this boat,"

said Anda, trying to steer Julienne away from the computer.

But the trip was doomed. The sky darkened as they left the house and the wind drew circles with the bus tickets and leaves. Halfway down the road, rain started.

"Oh, no! It's pouring."

They ran and crowded into a paper shop. David and Julienne started thumbing through computer magazines.

"It's not going to stop," sighed Anda. Between the Waffle and the flyover mist was closing in. Obviously rain had set in for the day.

"We'd better go home," said David.

"It's been blazing hot," said Anda. "Until you came, Julienne!"

"Never mind. We can play some of David's computer games," said Julienne.

Anda was disappointed. She'd wanted to treat them to a rowing boat. Failing that, she'd wanted to chat to Julienne and show her some of the difficult exercises Ian Barst had given her to do.

Julienne walked ahead, deep in conversation with David. Anda trailed gloomily behind, half tempted to go and hire a boat in the rain by herself. No, she'd be sensible. She'd go home and work at those exercises. At least she had Julienne now.

But to her annoyance, Julienne and David became instantly engrossed in the computer games.

"Don't you want to play, Anda? They're really easy!" said Julienne.

"No thanks. I just don't see the point."

Anda didn't want to be an oddball, but she couldn't muster any interest. There they sat all the afternoon, completely engrossed, while Anda wandered to and fro, doing her exercises half-heartedly, then furiously, on the soft carpet on the landing. Finally she leaned on her bedroom window sill and had a long conversation with a row of huddled pigeons.

By five o'clock she was mad with Julienne.

"She's *my* friend and she's come up to London to see *me*, not *him*," she told the pigeons angrily.

When she got Julienne to herself for a few minutes before tea she couldn't contain her rage.

"So you like David then!" she fired.

But the attempt at sarcasm was lost on Julienne.

"Yes I do. He's intelligent," she said.

"Not like me. I suppose I'm not worth spending time with now!"

"Don't be like that, Anda!" Julienne looked amazed. "I thought you'd be pleased we get on."

"I am. It's just that -- well — I haven't seen you for ages, and the first thing you do is get in with him and his wretched computer for the whole afternoon!"

Still Julienne would not be drawn. Anda hated herself for going on, but she couldn't stop.

"I've had enough!" she cried. "I wish you'd never come! I've had a bellyful in London. You've no idea."

Julienne looked hurt. "You wanted me to come! I'll go home again if you feel like that."

"No, Julienne, no. Don't be daft! Don't let's quarrel."

"Well you started it!"

Ill at ease with one another they went downstairs and helped Moira to get tea.

"I'm glad to see you're all getting on well," Moira said brightly. Obviously she, like David, had fallen under Julienne's spell. Julienne charmed everyone she met.

I can beat her at gymnastics, thought Anda, but not at being a person. Especially not now. And it was now that she most needed Julienne's friendship.

"You've changed, Anda," Julienne said later as they got ready for bed. "London's really changed you."

"How?"

"You're thinner, and you're older some how — and — and not carefree like you were. I don't know how else to describe it."

"Well I've never been away from home before. I've found it hard. London is so different. I think I really need to live in the country," said Anda, with an unexpected rush of homesickness. "I miss the Hooty Stream and the lovely fresh air. I even miss the sheep baaing."

"Have you told Moira?"

"No. No one."

"You should, Anda! Look at you. You're like a corked-up bottle. Moira would have been much kinder if you'd told her you were homesick instead of pretending to be so tough."

Anda shrugged.

"Maybe."

"That's why you're getting silly about me

making friends with David," said Julienne wisely. "You've been bottling things up. Just like I used to! Remember?"

"How could I forget?"

"My mum's much better since I stopped pretending to be hard. She's been really making an effort."

They talked far into the night. Long after Moira insisted on lights out they lay in bed giggling and swapping anecdotes. Julienne told Anda about her boring holiday in Wales and Anda vividly described her hard days of training with Ian Barst.

"I'll bet you win the eleven-to-thirteens championship at Ferndale after this!" said Julienne. "I can't wait to watch you, Anda."

"No — I shan't stand an earthly. Lena will win it again I suppose," said Anda realistically. But secretly she saw herself standing on the rostrum with a silver cup at Ferndale, with her friends and family clapping.

"It's three weeks tomorrow," said Julienne. "They've got an MRG section this time. I'm going in that."

"It'll be so lovely to be home."

"Are you bringing Ian Barst back as a garden gnome? He could sit by the Hooty Stream with a fishing rod."

That set them off giggling again.

The door opened and Moira came steaming in.

"Look, can't you shut up, you two? It's two o'clock in the morning! I need some sleep!"

"Never mind, Anda. I can't wait to come and

watch you training on Monday," whispered Julienne as they settled down to sleep.

"Me too."

But Julienne never did see Anda training. For Sunday afternoon proved disastrous.

All day Saturday, and on Sunday morning Anda became increasingly jealous at the way Julienne and David had ganged up, leaving her out. It wasn't intentional on their part, but most of their conversation was way above Anda's head. She felt uncontrollably angry. She wanted Julienne to be *her* best friend, the happy girl with plaits who had jumped the Hooty Stream with her and been her friend through the long hours of gymnastics at Ferndale. She even thought nostalgically of dear old Ferndale Gym Club. That happy disciplined atmosphere, with Christie's kind encouraging voice, seemed far removed from Ian Barst and his efficient echoing club. She sighed.

Not only had she lost Julienne, but David too. She couldn't believe both of them could be so disloyal.

She approached Julienne about it, but Julienne couldn't see why Anda should feel left out. Julienne was impossible to quarrel with. She'd always shrug her shoulders, smile and change the subject.

By Sunday afternoon Anda's black mood had mushroomed into a thundercloud.

"OK," she growled sullenly, when David suggested the rowing trip.

Past caring, she found her money and they set off for the canal.

"You don't have to treat us, Anda," Julienne said kindly. "We can all pay."

Anda shrugged.

"I said I would, so I will."

"What's up with you, Anda?" David looked at her, perplexed. "You're in a really bad mood."

"No I'm not! It's not a mood!" shouted Anda, furious at having her deepest feelings dismissed as a mere mood.

David backed off. He glanced at Julienne.

Anda saw the look between them and it made her even more furious. Homesickness and anger at Julienne gathered strength suddenly, like two jousting knights pounding towards each other.

"You two go ahead," she said curtly. "I want something from the shop."

"We'll come. What do you want to get? Sweets?"

"Nothing," growled Anda. "I just want to walk on my own."

She was almost crying. Julienne looked concerned.

"Whatever's the matter, Anda?"

"Nothing. You go on. I'll follow you."

Anda walked back towards the shop.

Leaning against a tree, she watched Julienne's bouncing curls disappear round the corner with David. No place of refuge! she thought savagely, wishing she could be teleported to her favourite spot high on the moors at home.

Where could she go here?

Nowhere!

She wandered up the footbridge, and stared down at the railway. Through a crack in the parapet she observed David and Julienne sitting in the willow tree waiting for her. Or were they? They wouldn't care if I never showed up, she thought angrily.

Sun glinted on the murky canal water. Anda turned to watch a train belting under the bridge and in that moment she noticed the girder. It drew her like a magnet. Of course. That's where she could go! On the girder! That would make them care.

She chilled. A wild horse galloped through her heart. Mentally she rehearsed a beam routine that could work on the girder, high above the water. A fall wouldn't be disastrous, she reasoned. It was only water. And she could swim enough to get out.

She sneaked down the steps and back along the canal to the girder before David and Julienne could notice her. She planned to wave to them from the middle of the girder! Oh yes, she'd make them sit up.

8

The Girder

She climbed like a monkey up the iron structure that supported the girder against the factory wall. Passing a window, she flattened herself against the wall. Supposing someone in the factory saw her? Unlikely, since it appeared dark inside. Perhaps the factory didn't work on Sundays.

The iron was rusty and stained her clothes. Lucky she was wearing old jeans and the dirty trainers that Moira hated.

With a rush of adrenalin she reached the girder. It was wider than a beam, at least twenty centimetres wide. Anda's eyes shone as she stepped on it. Four metres above the water. If I were not a gymnast, I'd be a bird!

The girder was firm under her feet. But just as David had warned, she felt disorientated being so high up. She sat astride it and took off her shoes and socks. Then she tied the laces together and hung them over the girder.

David and Julienne were still chatting in the

tree. Good. She didn't want them to notice her until she'd had a practice. Steady does it, I don't really want to fall, she thought, and walked across first to see how it felt. She tried to imagine blue crash mats underneath her, not cold water.

With a deep breath, looking straight ahead, she turned and ran back, her balance one hundred per cent. She tried a few dance steps and turns. Difficult on the slightly rusty surface. She did a few rolls to straddle. Easy. Now she could be more ambitious. Recklessly, she moved to the centre of the girder where she was over the water. Not daring to look down, she tried a walkover. Perfect. So perfect she did walkovers slowly all the way across. Lovely to be out in the sunshine, without Ian Barst shouting at her.

Exhilarated, she contemplated a back flip.

"Anda's a long time," said Julienne, swinging her legs round the willow tree.

David sat facing her.

"She knows her way around."

"Maybe we should go and meet her. She's in a funny mood," said Julienne, jumping down from the tree.

"I don't know what's the matter with her." David stayed in the tree. "She was all right until you came!"

"Thanks very much!"

"No, I didn't mean it like that!"

"She gets like this at home," said Julienne. "She has a blazing row with her mum and she goes off and does gymnastics on top of the hill!"

David frowned.

"Yes — she threatened to..." He looked up

and saw a tiny figure doing walkovers on the girder, four metres above the canal!

"Oh no!" he yelled. "Anda!"

Julienne stared in horror. Anda had done lots of mad things, but this had to be the worst.

"Crazy stupid, stupid little idiot!" roared David, giving full vent to his lungs.

"She can't hear us! We must get her down!" cried Julienne. "She must be stopped! Don't yell at her, David. You'll put her off balance!"

But David had gone running down the towpath like an angry bull.

"You idiot! Don't do it, Anda! Don't!"

"For God's sake!" Julienne hared after him.

Anda heard David's angry yell just as she took off for a back flip. She landed shakily, wobbled and almost fell.

Julienne screamed.

"Shut up, David. You'll make her worse!"

Shaken, Anda sat for a minute, astride the girder. She saw Julienne and David running down the towpath.

"I can do better flips than that!" she thought angrily.

She stood up, stretched and tried again.

"Anda! *No!*"

Perfect.

"Don't do any more!" pleaded Julienne.

"You get down here or I'll never speak to you again!" roared David.

But Anda was not stopping now.

Skilfully she did a walkover, followed by a flip. She'd intended to do two flips but something sharp on the girder caught her foot. It threw her right off balance.

Crack! Her skull slammed against the iron girder. The sun swung like a pendulum. The factory walls rushed past. Anda blacked out and fell like a rag doll into the canal.

A circle of ripples spread across the water where Anda had fallen. Julienne and David stared at each other.

"Do something!"

"She can swim!"

"But she cracked her head, David. I heard it! She's knocked herself out! She'll drown!"

"OK. Calm down." David was already stripping off his track suit.

Julienne was panicking.

"Help! Help us, somebody!" She shrieked at distant people walking along the towpath. But no one took any notice!

They waited for a moment for Anda to surface. But she didn't.

"Get her. Get her. She'll drown! How long does it take to drown. Three minutes?" cried Julienne. "I can help you if you can't lift her!"

David didn't wait any longer, but threw himself into the canal. He grimaced and dived beneath the surface. He had done his life-saving badge that summer, in a clean blue swimming pool. This was a deep and polluted canal! The water tasted foul. Bravely David opened his eyes and stared through the cloudy water. To his horror he couldn't see Anda. Help, where *is* she! he thought, shattered.

He shot to the surface.

Julienne was standing there barefoot, about to come in.

"Get help!" he roared. "No, don't come in yourself. I can lift her — I can't find her!"

"I'm coming in."

"No Julienne. You get help! Go on!"

David dived again.

Desperately, Julienne looked around. A middle-aged woman was walking her dog along the towpath. Still barefoot, Julienne sprinted up to her.

"Please, please help us. My friend's fallen in the canal. She cracked her head and we can't find her!"

Disbelieving eyes stared back at her.

"It's true, it's true. Please can you go and phone the police or ambulance. *Please.*"

"All right, dear. Where did she go in?"

"Up there."

A young man on a bicycle was coming along the towpath.

"I'll ask him. He'll go quicker," said the woman. "I'll come and help you."

"Thanks."

Julienne ran back.

She plunged straight into the water. It felt horrible. Freezing cold and stinking. She was bracing herself to dive when David surfaced, grim-faced, with one arm round Anda.

Her face was marble white, her body limp. Julienne felt the heat of panicky tears against the cold water. Anda was dead. And it's my fault! thought Julienne. My fault for ignoring her!

Poor, poor Anda.

Between them, they dragged Anda out on to the bank. David was swearing.

Gently he put Anda down on the grass.

"You don't put her like that. Put her like this. Oh no." Julienne was crying openly as she put Anda in the recovery position. "She could be dead."

"Is she breathing?"

"Her lungs are full of water."

Suddenly the woman with the dog took over, working expertly, with some urgency, to get the water out of Anda's lungs. Julienne and David watched helplessly.

"Pray," said Julienne, but she couldn't stop crying. She looked at David. "You were brilliant, rescuing her like that! I couldn't have!"

"I can hear a siren," said David.

The flashing blue light was so welcome. Suddenly an ambulance stood on the other side of the footbridge, and two ambulance men were running up the steps with a stretcher.

"She's breathing," announced the woman as Anda spluttered and drew hoarse faint breaths. "But she's had an awful crack on the head! They'll have to take her to hospital!"

"She could have fractured her skull!" said David.

"Oh don't, David, please!"

David's words registered in Anda's semi-conscious mind. A fractured skull! Hospital! What *had* she done? She fought to open her eyes.

Half of her was seeing Julienne, dripping wet, her hair plastered down, her eyes frightened like an owl in the dark. And the other half of her seemed to be walking up the lane to Hooty Cottage. She could see Bill in the garden tying beans, but she couldn't reach him. I'm still drowning. I'm still in the water, she thought.

Then she saw the ambulance men.

"No!" she cried, spluttering. "Don't take me to hospital."

A howling pain filled her head. She blacked out again.

"You go with her," said David. "I'll run home and phone Mum. And Anda's folks. I'll have to phone Gran."

Trying to keep calm, Julienne climbed into the ambulance with Anda, who lay on the stretcher like a sleeping Sindy doll.

"Thank you," she managed to say to the woman who had helped. "You've saved Anda's life."

"Don't worry, dear. They'll take good care of her."

The woman smiled kindly and walked off with her little dog, as if saving lives was an everyday occurrence.

David was running home, his lungs bursting, his track suit in his hand. He had saved Anda's life! In the back of his mind he was proud that he'd used his life-saving knowledge, proud of the courage he hadn't known he had. Momentarily he felt sad that his dad wasn't around to be proud of him. But Mum would be. And Gran!

What had been a disaster for Anda had actually sent David's self-esteem rocketing.

He arrived home and tore up the steps,

relieved to find he still had his door key safely round his neck. Knowing Moira would not be back until tea-time, he made a dive for the telephone.

And far away in Elmsford, in the quiet hum of a summer afternoon in Gran's garden, the sound of the telephone shrilled out of the window.

The Club Competition

"She'll need to rest for at least a week."

"We'll have to send her home."

That finished it, Anda thought, hearing the voices through fogs of pain, that was the end of her training with Ian Barst. I've really blown it. With a surge of fear, she remembered falling from the girder. Gingerly she moved her legs and arms. Nothing was broken. I'm in hospital, was the next panicky thought. She opened her eyes a discreet slit. Moira was standing by the bed, chatting to a smiling Irish nurse.

"I'm giving up gymnastics," she mumbled. At least I'm alive, she thought gratefully. To give up would be easy. A vivid picture of home came to her. She wanted desperately to go home.

"She's coming to at last!"

The smiling nurse leaned over her. She had such a merry freckled face and kind eyes that Anda couldn't help feeling safe with her, despite her fears about hospital.

"How do you feel, Anda?"

"I've got an awful headache. And my chest is wheezy," said Anda.

"You've got concussion. You'll be quite all right in a day or so. You lie quiet. I'll get the doctor to have a look at you."

"Doctor!" Anda looked startled. "What is he going to do?"

"Oh, don't worry! Only shine a little torch in your eyes and listen to your chest. That's all."

The nurse disappeared and Moira came to sit on the bed. She looked shaken and upset.

"Hey, don't worry, Auntie Moira! I'm sorry."

"I'm sorry too!" sobbed Moira, dabbing her face with a screwed-up tissue. "I know I should be bright and cheerful now, but I've been frantic about you, Anda. I was afraid you were going to be brain-damaged or something!"

Anda grinned reassuringly.

"My brain's not that brilliant anyway, so why worry!"

Moira was silent for a moment.

"You're a nice kid." She took Anda's hand. "And I know you think I'm a fusspot but I *do* care, you see. I'm sorry if you've had a rotten time in London."

Anda digested this in surprise. She had misjudged Moira.

"It's not been easy, bringing David up on my own," said Moira.

"No. I suppose it hasn't." Anda closed her eyes again. All this emotion was not exactly what she needed right now.

"Don't give up gymnastics," pleaded Moira. "You're so good. You'll get over this! And did you know David saved your life? He was a real hero!"

"And I was a silly fool," sighed Anda, "to dance on that girder. I'm sorry I've caused so much trouble. And please, please don't tell my parents!"

"We already have, Anda. We had to. They're on the way up here!"

"Are they mad?"

"No, of course not! And guess what?"

"What?"

"Gran has invited David down to stay for the last week of the holidays."

"Good! What about Julienne? Is she mad with me?"

"No. She'll be in to see you later. She was pretty shocked herself."

"I left my shoes hanging on the girder! Lynne'll go mad."

Worries loomed and flashed by like lorries on the motorway. What would Gran say? And Christie? Would she dare go back to Ferndale after this?

She did dare. Two days before the Club Competition.

A sunlit week at Hooty Cottage had restored her to full strength, and the dreadful incident when she had almost drowned had faded in her mind. London seemed like a dream. Ian Barst's voice had stopped barking in her head. She felt glad just to be home, to hear the bees and the stream, and to cuddle Bella's sun-warmed fur.

David was enjoying his week with Gran.

Impressed by his heroic rescue, Gran had made a fuss of him, and both were benefitting.

"It's time I got to know my brave grandson better!" she said, beaming.

As soon as Anda walked into Ferndale Gym Club on the Thursday evening, she felt truly at home. The atmosphere of a happy, well-disciplined gym club struck her instantly. It felt so friendly and welcoming that when Christie came and gave her a hug, she almost cried.

"We didn't expect you back so soon!"

"Hi, Anda!"

"Glad you're back!"

"We've missed you!"

All those dear faces surrounded her. Kerry, Elizabeth, John and Christie. And Julienne stood beside her, beaming. No one mentioned her embarrassing accident. And no one mentioned her not completing the course with Ian Barst. She felt profoundly grateful for their tact.

"This is David," she said brightly, pushing him forward. "He's a boy..."

Everyone laughed, and David bowed, enjoying the limelight.

"Yes, we can see that!" said Christie, smiling.

"A boy gymnast, I was going to say!" cried Anda.

"Oh! A boy gymnast! Marvellous! Come *in*!" John bounded forward. "We don't have enough of those around here! Are you going to give us a display on Saturday?"

David hesitated.

"We've got a pommel horse."

"And a high bar!"

"I think we've got some rings put away somewhere too."

"Oh go on, David!"

"OK." He looked pleased. "But don't expect much!"

"He's brilliant," said Anda warmly. "*And* he saved my life."

"Yes, I can't think why I bothered!" teased David and everyone laughed.

Suddenly everything fell back into place. It didn't matter whether Julienne was her best friend here. Everyone was friendly. Anda gave a sigh of happiness.

"And," she said to Christie, "I can do an eagle catch!"

"You can? That's marvellous! Come on then, let's get training."

The day of the Club Competition dawned golden and still. Everyone arrived early to help get the hall ready. Lynne helped arrange the mats and chairs. Gran sold programmes and gave out numbers and chatted brightly.

Anda didn't feel nervous. It was good to work with friends, rushing to lift this and straighten that. She helped Julienne with the little ones, tying their hair and listening to their worries and hopes.

Julienne was nervous, as always.

"At least you aren't competing!" said Anda consolingly. "It must be lovely just to do a display!"

"I wish I hadn't agreed to do it," worried Julienne. She was white-faced. She was to do two displays of Modern Rhythmic Gymnastics, one with a ribbon and one with a ball. As soon as they had all changed into best display clothes, she started agonizing.

"It's the ribbon one that worries me," she said. "If you don't get it perfect it looks awful."

"Well, what about me?" David reminded her. "Doing a display in front of a load of strangers. I haven't even prepared one!"

"People forgive you if you make a mistake in competition," said Julienne. "But they expect perfection in a display."

"Well I feel fine this time," confided Anda. "I'm not expecting to win anything. I'm just glad to be competing."

Julienne looked at her curiously.

"Mmm — you always used to be scared!" she observed. "Maybe Ian Barst has given you more confidence!"

"Maybe he has," said Anda thoughtfully, watching Julienne unwinding the long golden ribbon for her dance.

The audience assembled, hanging coats on chairs and positioning picnic bags. Gymnasts rushed about doing last minute warm-ups. John and Christie spotted tumbling runs on the mats.

Anda lingered by the table where all the trophies and medals were displayed. How she longed to win one, but she knew she wouldn't. Not today anyway. She had won medals, but never a silver cup. Longingly she fingered the coveted Club Challenge Cup with its list of names.

"I expect you'll be going home with that after your training scholarship!"

"Not today!" Anda turned to look at Lena. For once there was no animosity. Everyone knew Lena was likely to win the Club Championship.

Kerry was with her.

"Oh come on Lena! Don't be catty. Anda's only just out of hospital. She nearly died!"

"I wasn't being!" Lena smiled. "I wanted to be introduced to your dishy cousin!"

"What, David! Tough! He fancies Julienne!"

"He doesn't." Julienne rolled her eyes. "We're just friends!"

"Sh! We're starting!"

Christie came on to the stage with three important-looking visitors, two men and one woman.

"Who are they?" whispered Anda as the gymnasts marched in.

"The woman is a judge. The others are selecting for the county junior squad."

"Oh!"

Anda's heart raced. The county junior squad. She did some mental arithmetic. Was she old enough? Yes. Just. Experienced enough? No. Christie hadn't mentioned it to her. It was obvious they wouldn't pick her. She wasn't even at her best today! Forget it, she thought. But suddenly a huge wave of nerves washed over her.

"You've gone white!" said Julienne.

"So have you."

"We'll look like two ghosts marching in!"

There was no time to giggle.

"Look po-faced!" snapped John. "Everyone stand up straight. Tummies in! Off you go, Lena!"

Lena led the way in to the rousing march Christie always used. Suddenly they were gymnasts, po-faced and professional, not kids with feelings! Anda loved marching in, with the parents clapping. Her nerves felt grabbed together, as if she had left her stomach in the cloakroom.

As they stood in an immaculate line, she studied the faces of the two men who were selecting for the county squad. Was she imagining it, or was Christie pointing her out to them? I'm imagining it!

"ANDA BARNES!"

She stepped forward at the sound of her name, as they all did, and presented herself. Bill cheered loudly. He always supported Anda vociferously and she always felt good about it.

The competition day began with Julienne's MRG ribbon display. Beautiful and elegant in a white and gold leotard, she danced and rolled, sweeping the glittering ribbon into spirals and rings. She looked marvellous, but Anda was not envious. Julienne had had a hard time in gymnastics. She deserved success.

"Brilliant!"

Anda gave Julienne a warm hug when she came back from her display, flushed and happy. She hadn't dropped the ribbon.

"Yeah! Absolutely brill!" agreed David. "Really smart stuff!"

102

Julienne looked pleased.

"I'm starving now!" She smiled. "I'm going to pig sandwiches and watch Anda!"

The two older groups were beginning with bars and beam while the little ones did the floor and vault. Anda warmed up on beam with Kerry and the six others in her age group.

She didn't feel nervous. Or so she thought until she was presenting herself to the judge.

As she stepped on the beam she noticed the two county squad men, their faces a blur, looking up at her. Dancing and stretching, rolling, leaping and pirouetting, she went through her routine. Or tried to!

The fall from the girder had done something to her confidence. As she steeled herself for the walkover to back flip sequence, she had a sudden vision of London, its coppery sky twirling and the sound of Julienne's scream as the canal water rushed to meet her.

She fell.

"That's unusual for Anda!" said Christie.

Shaken and annoyed, she kept calm, getting straight up again. She took a deep breath. I can, she thought. But a shadow of pain in her head made her fall yet again, on to the blue mat. Humiliating!

"She's not right!" Lynne clutched at Bill's arm anxiously.

"I said she wasn't fit enough!" said Gran.

A wave of wanting to give up swept over Anda. Mechanically, she climbed back, but in her mind her legs were running out of the gym and across the lawn.

Silence fell as she balanced there, white-faced. Then with sudden kitten-like flexibility, she did it. A walkover and two flips. Shattered, she finished her routine and walked away, biting her lips, knowing she would have low marks and a time penalty.

Avoiding Julienne and David, she headed for the toilets and hid for three minutes. She stared at herself in the mirror.

"You will *not* fall apart. You will not," she instructed her shocked reflection.

But her bar routine brought the confidence flooding back. She managed her eagle catch. And everything else. With Ian Barst's voice ringing in her head, she achieved a magnificent back somersault dismount from the top bar.

"Oh my God!" Lynne shut her eyes.

"She *did* it!" cried Gran, clapping.

Bill cheered, Julienne and David clapped like windmills.

Pleased, Anda collapsed on a chair next to them for a welcome break.

"You have improved!" said Bill warmly.

"Improved!" Echoed Gran. "She's made *strides!* Well done!"

Anda smiled, pulling on her track suit. She looked at her mum.

"Don't tell me, Lynne," she grinned, "you shut your eyes!"

Lynne nodded sheepishly, handing Anda a cup of squash.

"I just can't watch!"

"Anyway, I've blown it with that beam

routine," said Anda. "I don't know what came over me."

But despite that, she felt happy, sitting in Ferndale with her favourite people. And she improved. Those gruelling weeks with Ian Barst had been worth it. And the beam work would come right again, she knew that.

So she relaxed and enjoyed the rest of the day. Her vaulting, Christie said, was excellent and gained her high marks. Her floor routine was snappy and beautiful. Claps and congratulations made a lovely change from criticism.

She gave a sigh of contentment.

The afternoon was nearly over. Soon it was time for Julienne's MRG ball display which she did with graceful ease. Then David.

Everyone sat up expectantly. Boy gymnasts were a rarity in Ferndale. Parallel bars and a pommel horse appeared. Then David came marching in, looking suddenly small and alone.

"He's scared!" whispered Anda.

"He's not!" said Julienne.

David managed to look very dignified. He began with a floor display. Not fast and brilliant like the girls, but slow, strong and controlled.

"He's good!" whispered Gran, her eyes shining. "I have two clever grandchildren!"

Next, a display on the parallel bars and on the pommel horse. Finally, David did two marvellous vaults. Everyone clapped and cheered enthusiastically.

"I never knew he was that good!" said Anda.

They made a fuss of David, who came back red-faced and bright-eyed.

"Great stuff!" said Bill, impressed.

David shrugged. But he looked pleased.

"They wouldn't think much of it in London," he said. "I don't often get clapped like that!"

"It does you good once in a while to get a bit of praise," said Bill. "I grow lovely beans and no one ever mentions it."

"Oh Bill!" Lynne started to say, when silence fell. The judges had added up the marks.

Quickly the gymnasts reassembled for final march in. As soon as they were all sitting in neat lines on the mats, an expectant hush fell, and the speeches and presentations began. Anda's heart throbbed. She tried not to think about winning anything.

First the medals. Kerry had one. Lena had lots! Time after time she seemed to be walking up for a medal. Anda looked enviously at her. She had *three*.

Then she heard Bill's loud cheer.

"Go on!" Kerry nudged her. "You've got first on the bars!"

Astonished, Anda jumped to her feet and walked out. She'd been too busy looking at Lena's medals to hear her own name! First on bars! She'd even beaten Lena, who was second!

Thank you, Ian Barst, she thought silently as she sat down, happily fingering the medal. You did this for me, even though I didn't like you!

But there was more to come.

Lena won the big Club Challenge Cup. Several other cups were presented to the younger members of Ferndale. Then Christie picked up a little bronze-coloured trophy of a dancing gymnast on a stand.

"And finally," she said. "We always present this one to the gymnast who has made the most progress in the past year. We call it the award for the most improved gymnast."

Kerry rolled her eyes at Anda and mouthed, "Lena again." Anda made a face. Then she heard Christie saying:

"Anda Barnes!"

She had won the little bronze trophy!

"I don't believe it," she muttered.

She smiled up at Christie. "I don't deserve it!"

"You do!" Christie smiled. She put a hand on Anda's shoulder. "And stay here a minute — we want you for something else."

Mystified, Anda stood, holding the precious statue. How super it would look in her bedroom! She beamed across at her parents.

The clapping died away, and silence fell again.

"We'd like Kerry up here please. And Lena," said Christie. "We've got one more announcement to make, and then you can all go home to tea!"

Kerry walked out, looking puzzled. She frowned questioningly at Anda. But Anda already knew! I daren't think it. I daren't! Emotions flooded through her. I shall cry, she thought crazily, if they've selected me. But I mustn't hope for it!

She dared not look at the two county squad men standing beside Christie. She hardly dared listen to the long speech one of them was making about the difficulties of selecting the right girls for the county squad. And she hardly believed her ears when he finally said:

"And today we have been lucky enough to find not less than three of these girls in Ferndale. We have selected for the county gymnastics squad: Lena, Kerry and Anda!"

Well that's it. I'm going to cry, thought Anda wildly.

The three girls turned and beamed at one another. They all cried. Then laughed. Then waved happily at the clapping people.

The clapping faded to a buzz of excitement. Parents mingled suddenly with the gymnasts. The golden sun of late afternoon glowed through the tall windows of the gym, and across the lawns of Ferndale.

Far away in London, the same sun lit the canal water as Moira walked home from work alone. On top of the footbridge she paused and looked down at the girder, astonished to see a small pair of shoes hanging there.

Anda's shoes, she thought. They'll be there for ever!

Some other Hippo Books to look out for:

THE LITTLE GYMNAST
Sheila Haigh

0 590 70407 9   £1.25

Anda has a natural talent for gymnastics and makes startling progress at the Ferndale Olympic Gymnastics Club. But Anda's parents are poor and gymnastics is an expensive hobby.

Will Anda have to give up her hopes of becoming an Olympic Champion?

THE ICE MOUNTAIN
Nicholas Walker

0 590 70780 9 £1.75

Benjamin certainly enjoys mucking around at the ice rink. But when someone suggests that he takes up ice dancing seriously — with stuck-up Belinda Thomas as his partner — he almost chokes on his shepherd's pie.

After all, ice dancing is for cissies .... isn't it?

SNOOKERED
Michael Hardcastle

0 590 70906 2   £1.50 (published March 1988)

What happens when you're a talented young snooker player with nowhere to play? Kevin Ashburn's struggle for recognition is tough, but can a chance meeting with a snooker professional give Kevin his lucky break!